Rowdy felt along the floor until his fingers closed upon a small rock. He sent this rock whizzing across the shaft; it struck the far wall and caromed; and Quong fired, his gun flash lighting the gloom and revealing him against the opposite wall. Rowdy fired, too, his shot blending with Quong's and stirring up thunderous echoes, but Rowdy felt that he had missed, too.

Rowdy glanced toward the dim entrance of the cave, which was almost invisible now, with the night gathering swiftly outside. No sign of Stumpy. But the situation within the mine hadn't changed; Quong was still there, his gun ready, and the Chinese must be double desperate now. . . .

Also by Norman A. Fox

ROUGHSHOD
LONG LIGHTNING
ROPE THE WIND

The Phantom Spur

NORMAN FOX

A DELL BOOK

Published by
Dell Publishing
a division of
Bantam Doubleday Dell Publishing Group, Inc.
666 Fifth Avenue
New York, New York 10103

The characters, places, incidents and situations in this book are imaginary and have no relation to any person, place or actual happening.

ISBN: 0-440-21052-6

Printed in the United States of America

Published simultaneously in Canada

July 1992

10 9 8 7 6 5 4 3 2 1

OPM

Contents

Across the sage flats, the road twisted like the tracks of a tipsy snake; and the stagecoach that was bearing those tireless travellers, Rowdy Dow and Stumpy Grampis, toward the cowtown of Tailholt bounded along this gone-to-grass highway in the manner of a jackrabbit late for an illicit rendezvous. It was no pleasure pasear. A summer sun hammered incessantly and malignantly upon the coach's roof; dust sifted through the curtained windows, and there were times when Rowdy and Stumpy were sure the wheels never touched terrain for miles at a stretch. On other occasions they were jolted so severely that their backbones tipped their hats down over their eyes. The man who survived such a trip deserved a medal—provided there was anything left of him upon which to pin it.

Against these exigencies of frontier travel, the trouble-shooting team had pitted a patient silence, even Stumpy, a great man for airing his likes and dislikes, quailing before the prospect of outshouting clattering wheels and thundering hoofs and the creak of thoroughbraces. But the third passenger had not bowed so ignobly to the destinies. Small and sixtyish, she was dressed in a manner that admitted of no nonsense; and she had silvery ringlets and shrewd blue eyes which peered through square, steel-rimmed spectacles. She had enlivened the miles with pointed remarks directed at Western roads, Western vehicles, and Western scenery.

"Land sakes!" she finally exclaimed. "It's not only bad

that there's nothing to see out here, but there's so much of it!"

Stumpy Grampis, suddenly touched by some obscure loyalty to the land, began to bristle. "If you don't like it," he observed, voicing the world's most irrefutable argument, "why don't you go back where you come from?"

The woman gave him a stare that would have curdled acid, measuring Stumpy with a disdainful eye; and Stumpy was something to see. A little man, fifty-odd, he had a leathery face and a look of having spent too much of his life in a saddle. Frost sprinkled his thinning hair and down-tilted moustache; and whereas he usually favoured garb that went with galloping, to-day he was got up in a manner that would have made his mother look twice to recognise him. Whereupon his mother would have promptly disowned him.

For Stumpy wore a chequered suit, a white waistcoat, a pair of yellow buttoned shoes, and a derby hat. He looked like a tobacco drummer fresh out of the makings.

"Sir," said the woman passenger, "I don't believe we've been formally introduced."

"That's easy remedied," said Stumpy. "Me, I'm——"

"Smith," Rowdy Dow hastily interjected. "Mr. Smith. He's one of the Smith boys."

Now Rowdy had been leaning back in his seat as indolently as a man might who was riding a thunderbolt, his eyes half closed, his mind busy with the mission that was bringing him and his partner into this corner of Montana—a mission that promised adventure and danger and perhaps a bit of profit. And Rowdy, erstwhile outlaw who packed a governor's pardon that was little over a year old, had reasons for keeping his lip buttoned. By this same token, it behoved him to be sure that Stumpy remained reasonably silent. His choir boy's face cherubic, Rowdy smiled. "And who do we have the pleasure of riding with?"

The little lady eyed all hundred and seventy pounds of Rowdy, taking in his bench-made boots, his foxed trousers and pearl-buttoned shirt. "I'm Miss Arabella Hatter," she said. "Of South Northwick, New Hampshire. I've taught English in the high school there these past thirty years."

"Ought to be turned out to graze!" Stumpy muttered.

Miss Hatter ignored him, still looking at Rowdy who was seated on the far side of the stage with Stumpy between the two. "And your name?" Miss Hatter asked.

Rowdy thumbed back his sombrero, thereby revealing black hair, inclined to curl. "Er—Smith," Rowdy said.

"A younger brother?" inquired Miss Hatter. "You can't be over thirty, Mr. Smith. Perhaps you two are related to some friends of mine in Poughkeepsie, New York. A pair of brothers. Whiskered fellows. They took over their father's business of manufacturing cough drops."

"Never make a go of it," Stumpy prophesied darkly. "Ain't enough consumers."

Miss Hatter looked at Stumpy with no great delight. "You're an authority, Mr. Smith? And pray tell me what is *your* business?"

Now it was to Stumpy's eternal sorrow that although he had spent most of his mature life riding the fringes of the owlhoot, the law had never adorned a reward dodger with his description. This had built a frustration in Stumpy that had caused him to scribble his name into the pardon the governor had bestowed upon Rowdy, but Stumpy's resentment still rankled. So now he said boldly, "I'm an ex-outlaw, savvy. A ring-tailed rannyhan that ain't never been curried below the knees!"

"Gracious!" said Miss Hatter. "You mean you followed a life of crime?"

"Followed it!" Stumpy bellowed. "Most o' the time I was three jumps ahead of it!"

Rowdy, again sensing that Stumpy might say the wrong thing at the wrong time, quickly swung the subject. "You're vacationing, Miss Hatter?"

"A combination business and pleasure trip," the spinster explained. She craned from the window and glanced across the endlessness of sage to where the Weetigo Range, off-shoots of the Montana Rockies, lifted above the north-western horizon. "You've heard, I presume, that Montana Central Railroad is building a spur into this section?"

Rowdy started. "Yes," he said, "we've heard."

Miss Hatter said, "As near as I can ascertain—and I've had voluminous correspondence with Montana Central's Chicago office—there was once a mining camp in the Weetigos called Porphyry. It flourished for a brief while, many years ago, and then became—what is it you Westerners call such a deserted village?—a spirit settlement."

"A ghost town," Rowdy corrected her.

"Yes, that's the term. But now new strikes have been made at Porphyry, and the railroad thinks it expedient to build track to haul away the produce of those mines." Miss Hatter frowned. "It so happens that I'm a stockholder in Montana Central. I bought three shares when the company was organised. So I told Mathilda—she's my room-mate; charming girl, teaches botany—that as long as I was thinking of going West to visit Cousin Lucius, and since I was going into the very section where the railroad was building, I might just as well look into matters. I've every right to know whether Montana Central is frittering away my investment on foolishness."

"Absolutely," Rowdy agreed.

Miss Hatter sighed. "Cousin Lucius really made up my mind for me. He simply insisted that I come and visit him this summer, and it was odd, his insistence, considering that we hadn't corresponded in a dozen years. Poor man, his handwriting looked so feeble. Let me see— Cousin Lucius was Uncle Ferd's oldest boy. That would make him better than sixty now. So I told Mathilda—we went to college together; she's really a charming girl—I said to Mathilda, 'Here's a splendid chance to kill two birds with one stone, don't you think?' Mathilda loves a well-turned phrase; sometimes I think she should be teaching literature."

"This Cousin Lucius lives hereabouts?" Rowdy inquired.

"He has a cattle ranch on the other side of Tailholt. I do hope he'll be on hand to meet me. But I imagine he will. He was so insistent that I bring the spur and made it a point that I bring it in person."

"The spur——?" Rowdy asked.

"Oh, yes. The old thing has laid around for years and years. It was about the last time that I corresponded with Cousin Lucius that I asked him to send me some trinket of the West. To place on the mantelpiece, you know. And he sent me the spur."

"Just one?" Rowdy asked. "They come in pairs."

"Gracious, so they do! Yes, there was only the one. I have it here in my bag." She indicated the carpetbag on the floor between her feet; she had insisted on carrying the bag rather than have it put in the luggage rack overhead as the driver had suggested at the station where the three had boarded.

"Odd," mused Rowdy.

"Seems to me I've heard tell of a cow-rancher up near the Weetigos named Hatter," Stumpy remarked. " 'Mad' Hatter, they call him. Nailed a horseshoe over his door for luck years ago, but it came down and caught him on top of the head. The feller's acted a mite queer ever since."

"Gracious!" said Miss Hatter. "Do you suppose that accounts for his making such a point about returning the spur?"

"Likely," said Stumpy. "Had an uncle once that was plumb unsettled in his mind. Thought he was a Christmas tree and was allus trying to get lit up."

"How interesting," said Miss Hatter. "Was he an outlaw, too?"

"Whole dang fambly has been curly wolves," Stumpy affirmed stoutly.

"You said you were an *ex*-outlaw," Miss Hatter reminded him. "If I'm not being too personal, what brought about your reformation?"

Stumpy put on a mournful mien. "I had me a lesson in human perverseness that plumb soured me on my chosen profession," he said. "Happened down in a little ole town in Wyoming. I'd been cutting me a wide swathe through them hills, leavin' death and devastation in my dust, till finally the fellers that made up my outlaw band just up and quit me outa mortal fear. They didn't have the nerve to folly in my tracks, them galoots. So I decided to rob me a bank singlehanded."

He paused to let the full effect of this sink in, and Miss Hatter asked with precocious interest: "Would that be an outstanding feat?"

"Outstanding?" howled Stumpy. "You think banks get robbed lone-handed every day? Why do you reckon Jesse James always had his brother Frank along? To hold his hankie and say, 'Blow hard'?"

"I'm sorry," said Miss Hatter. "This is all so new to me."

Somewhat mollified, Stumpy said, "I made my preparations careful-like, knowin' my career depended on it. I picked me a hitchrail near enough to the bank so's I could get back to that cayuse pronto, yet far enough away so's folks wouldn't wonder about a strange hoss being hitched handy to the bank. I picked my time careful, too, favourin' the noon hour when half the tellers would be out tying on the feed bag. I oozed into that bank and pulled off the slickest little hold-up you ever did see. And then I come backing out, not a shot fired, and that's when I run into calamity."

"The citizens had grown suspicious?"

"No siree," said Stumpy. "But while I was in that bank, doing an honest day's work, some misbegotten, unprincipled, thieving renegade of a son come along and stoled my hoss! It left me fit to be tied. Just went to show how rampant dishonesty is in this here world!"

Miss Hatter was silent for a long moment, frowning thoughtfully; and Rowdy, his face the epitome of innocence, looked like a man bursting inside himself. Then Miss Hatter said, "I'm sorry, Mr. Smith, but I'm forced to doubt the veracity of your story. I'm not a neophyte at the art of story-telling. In fact, I've had a few poems published in the South Northwick newspaper—*Odes to an Albatross,* I called them, inspired, of course, by the immortal Coleridge. I'm afraid your tale is too strongly based on the element of coincidence."

"Coincidence!" Stumpy shouted. "If that yarn ain't true, every word of it, I hope that this here stage stops so sudden-like that I fall forward flat on my face!"

Whereupon the stagecoach jolted to so sudden a stop that Stumpy was propelled forward into the space before the seat.

Rowdy was instantly craning his neck through a window; and by leaning far out, he saw what had caused the coach to stop. Seated upon a suitcase in the middle of the road was a man—a lone man in the midst of all this empty endlessness; and now the man was picking himself up and approaching to make palaver with the driver. Whereupon the man, obviously having persuaded the driver to accept him as a passenger, came around toward the stage door.

"Gracious me!" ejaculated Miss Hatter, who was also peering, "The man's Chinese!"

"A lot of them are being used as labourers on the Montana Central spur," Rowdy said.

But the man who climbed into the coach with a bland and apologetic smile was no coolie, imported from the West Coast to labour at the laying of rails and the pounding of spikes. Small and dapper, he wore a black suit of occidental cut; and his yellow, ageless face showed a definite intelligence. He said in a sibilant voice, "Extremely sorry to intrude." He placed his suitcase upon the floor and seated himself facing the three. "I seem to have been a victim of Western humour. My destination is the canyon country beyond Tailholt, and I was told at the last stop that it was within walking distance. I made the mistake of believing. Permit me to introduce myself. I am Doctor Quong."

"Doctor!" Stumpy, who'd picked himself from the floor, scowled suspiciously. "Where's yore black case?"

"I am not a doctor of medicine," said Quong. "I am a palaeontologist, and my degree was bestowed by one of your universities." His smile grew more bland; it was apparently a permanent fixture. "I am in search of dinosaur fossils. I have reason to believe that this country may reward my searching. I propose to organise an expedition. Are you perhaps interested in dinosaurs?"

"No," said Rowdy. "Never had any use for 'em."

The stage lurched forward; the clatter of hoof and wheel arose, and the dust came seeping again, and the thoroughbraces creaked, and it became difficult to make one's self heard above all this bedlam. And so silence held inside the coach. But something else was here now that cut off talk, and it was Doctor Quong. Whatever camaraderie had existed between the three was gone, now that a fourth had joined them, and it wasn't because Quong was an alien. Nor was it that the man was sinister in any way that could be defined. He was almost effeminate, yet his presence built a faint alarm in Rowdy that was made of instinct and bore no name.

Here, perhaps, was some sixth sense left over from outlaw days, and the tangled trail of Rowdy Dow had taught him to heed this sense. Thus he kept a certain watch on Doctor Quong as the miles unreeled, but the Chinese had wrapped himself in some dreamy reverie that made him constantly more remote. The sun still hammered, and the dust rose, and Rowdy mopped often at his face with his bandanna. Doctor Quong, apparently taking a cue from this, produced a white silk handkerchief and touched it to his yellow features, then let his hand lie idly in his lap, still holding the handkerchief.

Miss Arabella Hatter began to nod as the hours dragged by, and soon she was asleep. Stumpy, too, had been looking increasingly drowsier, and at last his head tipped towards Miss Hatter's shoulder, and then Stumpy's snores rose above the clatter. In all this, Rowdy found a contagion, and shortly he dozed. Intermittently he awoke to find Miss Hatter and Stumpy still sleeping. Doctor Quong had closed his eyes; he lay sprawled against the seat like a black spider.

Rowdy again craned his neck from the coach's window. Dust stung his eyes, and the wind batted at him; but he saw that the day was dying, the sun dipping towards the Weetigos; and those hills, though still many miles away, looked closer. This was new country to Rowdy, but he had made inquiries before climbing on to the stage, and he had a notion regarding the distance to Tailholt. Now he tried guessing at how many miles were left. They wouldn't finish their trip till after deep dark, he judged.

Reclining against the cushions, he fought off sleep. He would have liked to get out and stretch his muscles a little, but the coach had changed horses at a swing station many miles back, and Rowdy had been told there would be no other stop between there and Tailholt. He was shifting himself to a more comfortable position when the stage again jolted to a sudden stop.

The endlessness of the sage flats had been broken by a bluff and the coach had been running in the shadow of this for the last few minutes, and now the road had rounded the bluff, and three horsemen sat grouped by the side of the road. This Rowdy saw in a first hasty glance, and he likewise saw that all three riders had guns in their hands and bandannas pulled up over their noses. It was the threat of those guns that had pulled the stage to a stop. And now Stumpy and Miss Hatter, awakened by the jolt, were peering, too; and Stumpy drew in a long, hard breath.

"Land sakes!" Miss Hatter ejaculated. "Robbers!" She looked quickly at Stumpy. "Friends of yours?"

The stage driver, intimidated by the guns, was doubtless sitting his perch with his hands hoisted. The three horsemen yonder were alike in that each wore nondescript range garb; and they were alike, too, in the way they sat their saddles, tensely alert; but now one came down from his horse and stalked to the coach door on the side where Miss Hatter was seated. Without opening the door, the man peered inside. "You!" he barked, and the word was directed at the spinster. "Fork over whatever you're toting that spur in!"

Miss Hatter's hand faltered to her throat, anger and fear fighting to command her. "Gracious!" she cried. "What do you want with Cousin Lucius' spur?"

"Never mind," said the masked man. "Just pass it over!"

All this Rowdy Dow heard with only a corner of his consciousness, for crowding him hard were two thoughts. One was that against all reason he had suspected that calamity would befall them ever since Doctor Quong had come aboard. Yet Quong was making no overt move; he sat rigidly upright, his face inscrutable, the white handkerchief still in his hand. But Rowdy wasted no more than a glance on the Chinese, for Rowdy's second thought was that now there was a need for action.

2 ⋮ Girl with a Whip

At a time like this, Rowdy might well have nourished a third thought; for if he'd paused for proper reflection, he would have considered that here was no affair of his. Certain business had brought him to the Weetigo country, and that business involved a spur—but not the kind that might be used to scare a horse out of the hiccoughs. His mission had to do with the railroad spur being built to Porphyry, and thus he and Stumpy were travelling incognito, and thus Rowdy had started when Miss Arabella Hatter had mentioned Montana Central. But, faced with the preposterous proposition that three able-bodied men were bent upon stealing an object as worthless as a spur, Rowdy was taking cards.

The truth of it was that a great curiosity had consumed Rowdy; and, moreover, a sense of chivalry was prodding him. He had found an admiration for Miss Hatter across the miles, and he presumed that regardless of the value of the spur she was carrying, the little spinster doubtless resented the manner in which the spur was being wrested from her. Accordingly, Rowdy made his play.

He was seated nearest the door on the far side of the coach from which the outlaw had issued his order to Miss Hatter. With one quick movement, Rowdy wrenched open the door and fell out of the vehicle. At the same time he shouted, "Stumpy! Stay inside!" Rowdy wanted Doctor Quong watched, and there again instinct was working, and he hoped Stumpy would understand. Hitting the ground, Rowdy rolled under the coach; and as he rolled, he fired in the direction of the two masked horsemen who'd held back while the third was approaching the coach.

This much was to Rowdy's advantage; he had moved so quickly as to gain for himself the element of surprise. Yet he'd expected the one dismounted outlaw to fire at him as he'd hurtled from the coach. This man had stayed his trigger finger, but Rowdy was beating out a barrage that sent the outlaws' horses into a flurry of skittishness. They began rearing and prancing, voices rose in curses, and pandemonium was upon the masked trio. Rowdy sneered with professional scorn. These men had not prepared themselves for the unexpected, which indicated they were novices.

And now the stage driver was taking a hand. This was evidenced by his lifted voice; obviously the man had seized the opportunity when the outlaws had turned their attention to fighting their horses, and now a shotgun boomed throatily in the confusion. Rowdy's danger was that the stage horses might decide to take off while he was still under the coach. The driver had risked a grab at the gun, but the shot must have been wild; for Rowdy, rolling out from beneath the coach on its opposite side, saw no signs of carnage.

Rowdy was keyed to come to grips with the one dismounted outlaw, but that worthy had apparently lost all taste for this little tableau. His horse rearing and his companions having difficulty holding the mount along with their own, the third man was running to rejoin his fellows. He turned and his gun lifted, but a bullet geysered dust at his heels. He vaulted into the saddle.

Stumpy, who'd kept a six-shooter concealed somewhere about his outlandish garb, was now making that six-shooter speak, punctuating his shots with wild yells that further added to the confusion. And suddenly all the heart was gone out of the masked trio. Wheeling their horses about, they made fast tracks; and Rowdy found himself on his hands and knees beside the stagecoach with no target but a dust cloud.

He came to a stand. Stumpy, peering from the window, shouted, "We licked 'em, Rowdy, old hoss! We made 'em hit the grit!"

Rowdy glanced up at the driver, a grizzled man so long associated with horses that he was beginning to look like one. The driver, who'd been jamming a fresh cartridge into his shotgun, had set the gun aside to take the reins and fight the fractiousness of his own horses, which had found the skittishness of the outlaw cayuses a contagion. The driver spat with great disgust. "Helluva show," he observed. "I mind the time when a man could get a mite o' fun outa being held up."

Rowdy dusted himself off. "We'd better get rolling."

He climbed back into the stage, concerned now for Miss Hatter. She had just had a taste of Woolly West, and he was afraid that she might have fainted; but he found her sitting bolt upright, her blue eyes shining behind the steel-rimmed spectacles.

"Gracious," she exclaimed, "I was having one of my headaches till all this happened. Now it's gone." She frowned, glancing out of the window to where the fast-moving dust cloud that marked the trio's departure grew smaller. "I just wish I could have laid my parasol across the heads of those uncouth fellows!"

Doctor Quong looked as though he'd turned not so much as a hair in the interim. "My congratulations," he said with a show of his teeth. "That was indeed quick thinking and quick shooting you displayed. I owe the safety of my lowly possessions to you."

"Forget it," said Rowdy.

The stage suddenly jolted forward, and the trip was resumed. But Rowdy hadn't yet cased his gun, and for a long time he held it in his lap, his eyes on the horizon toward which the three had headed, until the descending dusk obscured his vision. Curiosity still prodded at him; he was trying to fathom why the hold-up had been directed against the spur Miss Hatter carried, and he was toying with the notion of boldly asking her about that when the spinster said, "Now why do you suppose those men wanted Cousin Lucius' old spur? Land sakes, it doesn't make a bit of sense!"

"I wonder," Rowdy said.

The night came quickly, a moonless night of deep dark that wrapped the rangeland in its arms and squeezed it tight; and inside the coach the four passengers could no longer see each other. In due course this darkness throbbed to Stumpy's snores; the little man had again dozed off; but Rowdy held to alertness, reasoning that a second hold-up might be attempted. His hope was that the outlaw trio had got such a bellyful as to be discouraged for the night, and he breathed easier as the last miles unreeled. They were drawing close to Tailholt, and thus the chances of a second attack diminished.

They reached the cowtown near the midnight hour, Stumpy rousing himself grumblingly and Miss Hatter stirring to wakefulness, too, as the stage came clattering into town to draw up before the depot. Again there was that bone-jolting lurch, and then they were at journey's end.

Miss Hatter peered from the window and said sleepily, "So this is Tailholt."

Rowdy, also peering from the window, was trying to get an impression of the town. Tailholt was no metropolis, though its hitchrails were crowded and its boardwalks teemed with humanity. Two rows of false fronts faced each other across a ribbon of dust that was the street. Once a cowtown, Tailholt had sat down in the sun and fallen fast asleep; and if the settlement by any stretch of imagination could have been considered as a Sleeping Beauty, then Montana Central had given it the clangorous kiss that had awakened it. A constant roar emanated from the town, like a dragon with its tail being twisted; and though spurs jangled along the boardwalks, the heavy boots of railroad construction workers beat a tattoo also. And the Chinese were here as well, drawn by their perpetual penchant for gambling. A switch-engine hooted on a siding; an engine bell kept up a monotonous clanging. All in all, Tailholt was nothing to soothe the nerves.

"Danged town's got the St. Vital dance," Stumpy observed.

He was out of the coach and assisting Miss Hatter to the boardwalk. Rowdy dismounted; and Doctor Quong came after him, giving the group his bland smile, then shouldering into the crowd and making himself scarce.

Miss Hatter looked around. "Dear me," she said, "it appears that nobody's on hand to meet me."

"Hotel across the way," Rowdy observed. "We'll take you there."

Stumpy hoisted Miss Hatter's bag and also took the carpetbag with which he'd provided himself, in keeping with the strange garb he'd chosen to wear. They crossed the street at considerable risk; huge freight wagons threaded this narrow way, the drivers pouring such shocking language upon their horses that Stumpy, the possessor of a sulphuric vocabulary himself, had to pause in openmouthed admiration. When they'd gained the far boardwalk, they turned in at the Traveller's Rest and presented themselves before the desk clerk. Miss Hatter signed quickly; and when a room was indicated for her, she gave the partners a weary good night and made off.

Rowdy said, "We might as well sign up, too," and put the names of Smith and Smith upon the register.

The desk clerk regarded Stumpy affably. "Drummer?" he inquired. "What's your line?"

"Smoke," said Stumpy, sourly.

"Ah, cigars . . ."

"No," said Stumpy. "Gunsmoke."

Rowdy looked at the number on the tag attached to the key. "Put Mr. Smith's bag in our room," he ordered the clerk. "We'll have a look at your village. By the way, where would a man find Mark Champion?"

"Down the street," the clerk said. "The railroad people have taken over the Odd Fellows hall as offices. Champion may be around there; then again, he may be out at end-of-steel. Are you railroaders?"

"They might be hiring somebody to tote water to the working boys, now mightn't they?" Rowdy asked.

He and Stumpy shouldered out into the street, Stumpy limping slightly in his yellow buttoned shoes and cursing under his breath. Around them the town roared, a sleeplessness to it, and Rowdy said, "That high-looking building yonderly might be railroad headquarters. Come on, Stumpy. We might as well let Champion know we're here."

"I want a drink," Stumpy announced.

"*A* drink, Stumpy?" Rowdy inquired sceptically, knowing his partner's weakness.

"Maybe two," Stumpy admitted. "Me, I been exposed to the rigours of travel which would a' wore a lesser man down to the nub. Consarn it, Rowdy, I'm entitled to a moment of relaxation."

Rowdy sighed. "Very well," he said.

But the malignant destiny that had shadowed most of Stumpy Grampis' days decreed that he was to have no drink this night. For as the partners elbowed their way along the teeming boardwalk in the direction of the nearest saloon, their attention was suddenly drawn to a group of men bursting from that same saloon, a huddled tightlipped group surrounding a figure they seemed to be half-carrying, half-dragging along; and the man in the lead had a coiled lariat over his arm. It didn't take a second glance to tell that this was no quilting bee.

"A lynching!" Stumpy breathed. "They're going to hang that jasper!"

The group had spilled into the street and was heading away from the partners, and Rowdy saw that all these men were of the bow-legged breed, cattlemen and cowboys, and they made a silent, intent crowd. There should have been cursing and lifted voices and perhaps the popping of guns, but they were going about their business the quiet way. And suddenly Rowdy was dragging at Stumpy's elbow, hurrying his partner along. "Come on," Rowdy cried. "This thing needs busting up!"

Once again he might have taken time to reflect that here was no concern of his, yet all the indications were that a lone man was to die at the hands of the many; and Rowdy, who'd known what it was to have a rope around his neck, could no more have helped interfering than a steer could resist salt. The group ahead was moving swiftly; and Stumpy, attempting to run, fell into an awkward limp. Rowdy tugged hard at his partner. A freight wagon loomed up, blocking the way; and they lost sight of the lynchers, and then they glimpsed them again. Those men were heading for the outskirts of town, and they were putting distance between themselves and the puffing partners.

But Rowdy and Stumpy were hurrying as fast as they could, and now the buildings were thinning out, and the two were at the town's outskirts; and here a huge cottonwood loomed, black and many-armed, against the night sky. The group had converged beneath this cottonwood; and even as the partners came charging up, a rope sailed over a lower limb and a figure rose at the end of that rope, a figure that twisted and turned but did no struggling. And Stumpy, sobbing from exertion and a sense of defeat, cried, "Dang it all! We're too late, Rowdy!"

But Stumpy at the same time was getting his gun from cover, and he came charging among the astonished cattlemen, flourishing that gun. "Cut that jigger down!" Stumpy barked. "Cut him down whilst he still can wiggle!" And then both Rowdy and Stumpy were beneath the tree, staring upward, staring in startled disbelief; and Rowdy said in a dazed voice, "Why, it's a dummy!"

For, just as sure as shootin', the thing suspended at

the end of the hang-rope was no more than a man's suit, surmounted by a huge hat, the suit stuffed with rags or straw; and Stumpy stared about wildly, obviously trying to make sense out of something so strange as this.

"Look, feller," a grizzled cattleman said, "That there strawman represents Big Tom McMasters, savvy. We're hanging him in effigy. We've been doing it once a year now for thirteen years—always on this same night."

"What did the jigger do to get hisself hung thirteen times?" Stumpy demanded.

"Thirteen years ago to-night he walked out of the bank he was running here," the cattleman said. "And when he walked out, he took every cent the bank had in its vault. That was our money, savvy—the money we'd trusted the thievin' skunk with. Just about busted this range, Tom Mc-Masters did. We never caught up with him to give him a real hanging, but we have our little fun makin' a play at it on the anniversary, just to keep ourselves reminded of Tom."

"Jumpin' Jehoshaphat!" Stumpy exclaimed. "A dummy!"

There had been belligerence in this crowd, an indication that they hadn't appreciated this intrusion upon their private party—especially by a man in a drummer's duds. But now the laughter went up, for here was a kind of humour these cattlemen of the Weetigos could understand. Stumpy silently put his gun away, his face looking like something that had been caught in a whirlwind. Rowdy stared upward at the inanimate thing that represented Big Tom McMasters and tugged again at Stumpy's elbow.

"Come on," Rowdy said. "The joke's on us."

They turned away, the laughter of the pseudo-lynchers following them; and when they came back along the street, they saw that all their luck had clabbered. They found the Odd Fellows building, and they learned that the railroad offices occupied the second story, over the town's bank, but the entire building was dark. Rowdy sighed. "Might as well go to bed."

Stumpy, so disgruntled over having dashed to the rescue of a dummy that he'd forgotten his desire for a drink, nodded. "Me, I could use a bed," he admitted.

And so they came again to the hotel, got their key, climbed to their room and admitted themselves; but sleep was not yet for them. The room looked like a hundred others; there was a bed that appeared to be on the verge of collapse, a bureau with a pitcher and bowl, a chair or two, and wallpaper that would have driven a bull to a fighting frenzy. But the bed looked reasonably inviting.

Rowdy had just got the lamp lighted when the door burst inward. Rowdy swung, his hand dropping toward his cased gun. It was a girl who stood glaring at him.

"Well," she said. "Where is it?"

"Where's what?"

"The spur!" the girl snapped, and that was when Rowdy noticed the whip.

It was a mighty big whip for such a little girl to be carrying, a huge bull whip such as freighters favoured, but no man at first glance was going to see the whip. Not so long as this particular girl was carrying it. No more than nineteen, she wasn't much bigger than a minute, and she looked boyish in Levis and shirt, but she had long black hair that tumbled to her shoulders, and her face was altogether breath-taking, for she was big of eye and red of lip —a very pretty, very angry girl.

Rowdy said, "Would you mind telling us what you're talking about?"

Stumpy made a move to cross the room, and instantly the whip uncoiled and flicked out, the lash whistling to cut the air no more than an inch from Stumpy's nose. Stumpy froze with a howl.

"I'm Taisy Hatter," the girl announced stonily. "I've just come to town to fetch my aunt to our ranch. I found her in quite a stew. While she was aboard the stagecoach, somebody got into her luggage and removed a spur she was carrying. There were just three other passengers. And one of them got that spur!"

"Doctor Quong!" Rowdy ejaculated in sudden understanding.

"More likely one of the Smith boys!" The girl's lip curled contemptuously. "You won't fool me the way you fooled my aunt. She said you two called each other Rowdy and Stumpy. Do you think I've never heard of Rowdy Dow and Stumpy Grampis? You wanted that spur so bad you fought off outlaws that likewise wanted it. Now you're going to hand it over. Or I'm going to take the hide off both of you!"

3 : Trouble-Shooters

History has indicated that there are times for peaceable discussion and times when the cannon must roar, and though Rowdy was no great student of such matters, he knew that palaver now would be pointless. This girl, Taisy, had added her own two and two and arrived at a conclusion as solid as stove lids. A single-minded wench if there ever was one, she was sure the partners possessed the stolen spur. Moreover, she had a bull whip and a temper, and Rowdy suspected he might soon feel the cutting edge of both. To save himself from this, he was supposed to produce a spur that had become a will-o'-the-wisp, a phantom spur that had gone with the night wind.

Whereupon Rowdy gave up any thought of diplomacy and went into action.

He wanted that whip out of Taisy's hand, but he didn't try rushing her. Instead he shouted, "Watch out, Stumpy!" and darted across the room, darted in the direction of the bureau upon which the lighted lamp perched. Again the whip flicked out; Rowdy felt the hot touch of it upon his shoulder, and the whip withdrew to lash out again. But Rowdy had reached the bureau, and he blew out the lamp with one quick *whoosh,* then fell to the floor and rolled. Stumpy was moving somewhere about the room; the whip was frantically searching the darkness, but Rowdy came up against Taisy's Levi-clad legs and wrapped his arms about them, spilling the girl to the faded carpet.

Here was fighting that called for its own special rules; no gentleman could bust a lady one on the beak. Sweating mightily, Rowdy managed to pinion the girl's arms to her sides, and he judged that she let go of the whip then, for when she broke free she clawed at him with both hands and even used her teeth. She made quite a handful; but Rowdy got to a stand, dragging Taisy to her feet, and he panted, "Light the lamp, Stumpy!"

Stumpy said, "You plumb sure it's safe? This here room is full of catamounts!"

He got the lamp glowing again, and Rowdy looked at the struggling, dishevelled girl in his arms. "Listen," Rowdy said sternly, "we haven't got your aunt's spur. It must have been taken out of her luggage after deep dark settled down; for a while you couldn't see your hand in front of your face in that stagecoach. Now do I have to shove you out into the hall and lock the door after you, or will you leave like a lady?"

Taisy's eyes were stormy. "You win this hand," she said. "You thieving scoundrel!"

Rowdy sighed. "Heave up the sash and drop that whip out of the window, Stumpy. Our guest can pick it up after she leaves."

Stumpy gingerly took the whip from the floor and did as he had been directed. Rowdy released the girl. She stood for a moment, shaking with anger, glaring at both of them. Then her lips quivered. "You b-big b-b-bullies!" she cried and darted into the hall.

"Whew!" said Rowdy as he closed the door.

Stumpy said, "We should never have come to this Weetigo country, Rowdy. I've felt it in my bones from the fust. By grab, the women folks hereabouts is regular *amulets*!"

"You mean, Amazons. Go to bed, Stumpy. I'm going to have a little look-see."

"Rowdy!" Stumpy said admonishingly. "You ain't aiming to go sparkin' that gal? She's mighty purty, and it seemed to me you kept holding on to her a mite longer than was necessary."

Rowdy fingered his scratched cheek reflectively. "If I see her coming, I'll climb the handiest cottonwood. Go to bed, partner. I'll be back soon."

And he was, though Stumpy was snoring loudly and occupying the lion's share of the bed when Rowdy tiptoed in a half hour later. Rowdy, locking the door, eased himself into the bed and thus it was not until they were washing up the following morning that he made his report.

"I went down to the wagon yard," Rowdy said. "The stagecoach was there; it doesn't make another run till today. I spent quite a few matches, but I found what I finally figured I might find. Just a wisp of fine silk caught in a splinter on the side of the stagecoach."

"What's that got to do with the price o' beef in Boston?" Stumpy demanded sourly.

"Our friend, Doctor Quong," said Rowdy, "had a white silk handkerchief in his hand most of the time he was aboard the stage. The sign says he must have had his hand outside the window part of the time. That's why a bit of silk got snagged by that splinter."

Stumpy's hairy ears perked. "Then he was signalling?"

"Right as rain," said Rowdy. "To those three galoots who stopped the stage. Quong is no fool. He wouldn't have been walking the flats just because he was told it was only a hop and a skip to Tailholt. He wanted aboard the stage and I'm betting he was out there on a horse, along with his three friends, until he decided to pretend he was stranded. He got on the stage to make sure that Miss Hatter was aboard. Once he was sure, he waved to his three friends to close in."

Stumpy's face puckered with thought. "And when we drove off them jaspers, Quong made his own private play for the spur—something he didn't want to risk doing unless he had to."

Rowdy nodded. "That's the way I figure it. Those outlaws didn't fire a shot. That seemed odd to me at the time.

Now I savvy. They couldn't go throwing lead around as long as Quong was in the stage."

"Where do you reckon Doctor Quong is now?" Stumpy asked.

Rowdy shrugged. "He's not registered here. I looked last night. And we can't waste time hunting him. We've got business of our own. We'd better be finding Mark Champion."

But first they had breakfast, wincing at the price they had to pay; for with the coming of the railroad construction crews, Tailholt had turned into a boom-camp. They saw no sign of either Miss Arabella Hatter or her whip-wielding niece this fair morning, and shortly they came along Tailholt's busy street to the Odd Fellows building, found a stair and climbed to the floor above.

A pale, bespectacled clerk sat at a desk in an anteroom at the head of the stairs, and to him Rowdy said, "Mark Champion about, mister?"

The clerk looked over the pair with no noticeable enthusiasm. "He's in conference," he announced. "You'll have to come back."

"Thanks," said Rowdy and started for a door giving off from this anteroom.

He got the door open before the startled clerk could make a try at stopping him, and he stepped into a long room with a conference table centering it. At one end of this table sat three men and a small boy. Rowdy had a look at the man at the head of the table, and here, he decided, was Mark Champion. Champion sat in his shirt sleeves, a youngish man, bronzed by many suns, his sandy hair and eyebrows faded by those same suns. There was a frank, friendly openness to Mark Champion that Rowdy liked, albeit Champion was frowning at this intrusion.

Rowdy said, "I'm Rowdy Dow. And this is my partner, Stumpy Grampis."

Champion's look turned to one of utter amazement as

his glance shifted to Stumpy, who was again wearing the chequered suit, the yellow shoes and the derby hat.

"I don't believe it!" Champion breathed.

"Me, neither," said Stumpy. "But we was told to come to Tailholt incognito. I looked the danged word up in a dictionary. It has a whole passel of meanings, but one of 'em said something about a state o' being disguised. These here dude duds is a disguise."

"Incredible!" gasped an extremely huge, florid-faced, over-dressed man with a shining bald head, who sat at Champion's right. The big man gave Rowdy and Stumpy a look that indicated his utter bewilderment. "Champion," he said, "who are these people?"

Champion came to his feet and proved to be a tall, well-built man. "Excuse me," he said, and, to Rowdy and Stumpy: "Gentlemen, allow me to present Bartholomew B. Bartholomew, third vice-president of Montana Central. He's out here on a special trip to discuss some of our difficulties. B.B., these men are here to take on the work of trouble-shooting for us. And from what I've told you, you'll agree that we drastically need some trouble-shooters."

The boy was seated next to Bartholomew, a lad of no more than ten, with the most angelic face Rowdy had ever seen. He was wearing a lace-trimmed Lord Fauntleroy suit of black velvet, and he had yellow curls which fell to his shoulders, but the angelic effect was instantly lost as he screwed up his face and gave the partners a grimace of derision.

"Nyah!" said the boy. "They don't look so capable."

"Launcelot!" Bartholomew cried reprovingly. "My son, gentlemen. I brought him along to see the construction end of railroading. Some day he shall succeed me to my position with Montana Central."

"He needs a paddling!" Stumpy decided.

Bartholomew B. Bartholomew looked exceedingly pained. "Mrs. Bartholomew and I have never felt that children should be repressed in their natural tendency towards frankness, sir."

"You tell 'em, *pater*!" Launcelot applauded.

The third man at the table said, "I'm not so sure but what the boy's estimate is accurate."

Here was a thin, stoop-shouldered individual clad in rusty black, a man long of face and long of sideburns, with a gimlet-eyed, long-nosed look to him that automatically suggested debits and credits. Champion said hastily, "May I present Abner Grubb? Mr. Grubb is the local banker and has been most co-operative in helping our work along. Mr. Grubb, I'm sure you've heard of Rowdy Dow and Stumpy Grampis."

"Yes," said Grubb, "I've heard of them. Mr. Dow's picture long adorned the Tailholt post office, along with a description of him and the offer of a sizable reward. I've never approved of the governor's laxity in pardoning him, in spite of public acclaim. As for Mr. Grampis, he seems to be cut from the same undependable cloth."

"Outlaws?" said young Launcelot with greater interest. "I don't believe it. "Where's their masks?"

"Look," said Rowdy with some heat, "I didn't come here to be pinned on a card like a butterfly. Last fall, me and Stumpy did a few chores in Latigo Basin. There we met a young gent named Logan MacLean, who'll do to ride the river with. He's an official of Montana Central, as you damned well know."

"Of course," Bartholomew nodded. "A very up and coming young man, MacLean."

"Late this spring, me and Stumpy finished up a job in the Bearclaw country," Rowdy went on. "Not long after, we were wetting our whistles in Kalispell one night when we ran into MacLean. He'd stopped there on business, him and his wife. He asked us if we'd be interested in a job. His friend, Mark Champion, was running a spur to Porphyry and having a heap of trouble. MacLean said he'd write you, Champion, and tell you we'd lend a hand; and he suggested we head for Tailholt incognito. We've been Smith and Smith up till this morning. We're here because Logan MacLean happens to be a good friend of ours. We're not standing here with our hats in our hands begging for a job. Good-day, gentlemen!"

"Wait!" Champion cried. He cast a hasty glance at Abner Grubb. "I'm sorry you feel as you do about these men, Grubb. I've appreciated the support you've given us, especially in trying to bring Mad Hatter to our way of thinking, and I wouldn't want to lose that support, but——"

"Of course, I've supported the railroad," Grubb interjected. "It will mean greater prosperity to this range; and, as a banker, I will prosper along with the Weetigo country. I don't mean to dictate your personal policy, Champion. I'm just not sure it's wise to put your trust in men who so recently rode beyond the law."

"We're bucking lawlessness," Champion said. "We've had agitators in our construction crews and long-riding men lifting our payrolls, and we've had property destroyed. That sort of thing can't be handled with kid gloves. Dow," he looked at Rowdy. "I'm grateful to MacLean for sending you to me, and I'm grateful to you and your partner for coming. If you'll take the job, I'll be even more grateful."

Bartholomew cleared his throat. "I'm not sure but what I'm inclined to Mr. Grubb's point of view," he said.

Anger put crimson in Champion's cheeks. "This isn't Chicago," he said tartly. "And our problems aren't problems of the desk. You've bestowed some authority upon me, B.B. As chief construction engineer, I'm using that authority to hire these men if they wish to be hired. Dow, what do you say?"

It was characteristic of Rowdy that he made his decision quickly. Stumpy was frowning; and Stumpy, Rowdy judged, would have elected to walk out on this group; but Rowdy said, "You can put us down on the payroll." And even as he said it, he knew it was his dislike for Abner

Grubb that prompted his decision. The man had bucked them, and now with a certain perverse delight Rowdy was bucking Grubb. He watched the banker's long face, but Grubb was not to be read.

"We now appear to be in the same camp," Grubb said with no great graciousness. "If Mr. Champion chooses to employ you, then you'll find me co-operative."

"Thanks," Rowdy said dryly.

"Ought to have his long nose rubbed agin the floor," Stumpy opined low-voiced.

Rowdy looked at Mark Champion. "You've already given me an idea of the troubles you're up against. It would seem there's an element opposed to your putting the spur through. Is there anything special that's giving you the greatest grief?"

"Yes," said Mark Champion and suddenly was a tired man who had to seat himself, and about him there was the look of one dealing with the impossible. "Yes, we have one special trouble that's made all of us doubt our sanity. Dinosaurs, Mr. Dow. Dinosaurs."

4 ⋮ Launcelot on Dinosaurs

Now enough had happened to Rowdy Dow since he'd come to the Weetigo country to convince him that this land was loonier than a bedbug on a binge. First there'd been the stagecoach ride, with Miss Arabella Hatter speaking of her Cousin Lucius, more commonly known as Mad Hatter, and the spur the man craved. Then Doctor Quong had appeared in the middle of nowhere, and thereafter masked men had tried to wrest the spur from Miss Hatter. Thus Rowdy had had a taste of the fantastic before he'd set eyes on Tailholt, and the town itself had held its share of surprises. The men hereabouts were given to the hanging of dummies. And the girls—bless 'em—toted bull whips and showed an alarming dexterity at the use of them.

Moreover, Rowdy had had his equilibrium slightly upset when he'd appeared here in this conference hall expecting to be welcomed with open arms to the payroll of Montana Central. Instead he'd found opposition on every side. All of this added up to enough surprises to make a man's head buzz, but Mark Champion's last remark was the corker that capped the climax.

Whereupon Rowdy dredged up a weak and hollow laugh. "Do you know," he said to Champion, "I would have sworn you just said you were troubled with dinosaurs."

The chief construction engineer showed no signs of amusement, his sunburned face creasing with a frown. "That's exactly what I said," he affirmed. "Look——" He drew from the centre of the table a large map and spread it out so Rowdy could see. The map showed the railroad moving in from the south-east and extending to Tailholt and beyond the town. Champion's finger touched the map to the north-west of Tailholt.

"Here's a stretch of canyon country," he said. "We're laying track through it right now. Beyond"—his finger moved—"is the Hatter ranch, and beyond that lie the Weetigos and Porphyry, our goal. We're having trouble with Hatter—he doesn't want to allow us right-of-way across his range—but the big problem right now is to get through the canyon country. Because that's where the dinosaurs are bothering us."

Rowdy studied the map. "What's this Humpback Hill on the other side of Hatter's ranch?"

"The only large obstruction that lies between us and the Weetigos, once we're beyond the canyons. We'll tunnel through Humpback. Our engineers looked over the country months ago and decided that was the most feasible way to conquer the hill."

Abner Grubb said, "I'm not acquainted with the engineering factors, but I still think you'd be wise to by-pass both Hatter's place and Humpback Hill. Even if it means laying miles of extra track. I tell you, Hatter is stubborn."

"These dinosaurs," Rowdy said warily. "They're pretty bothersome?"

"You're laughing, Dow," Champion observed, "and I can't say that I blame you. The canyon country is weird at best. Of late we've had several thunderstorms, and each time our construction crews have stampeded, swearing they've seen huge forms lumbering through the night. The workers are an ignorant, superstitious lot; and I wasn't much impressed at first. Then my construction boss, Avalanche McAllister, caught a glimpse of one of the monsters and drew a rough sketch for me. It was surprisingly like a Tyrannosaurus. And the description furnished me by the more coherent workers on other occasions indicated that they'd seen a Brontosaurus."

Stumpy nudged back his derby with a frown. "Make up your mind," he said sourly. "I thought you said dinosaurs. Now you're claiming the boys saw these other critters."

"Dinosaurs," said little Launcelot in a very bored voice, "are any of certain extinct land reptiles of the Mesozoic era. The word itself is from the Greek and means terrible lizards. Under the general classification come certain carnivorous bipeds, such as the Tyrannosaurus, herbivorous quadrupeds like the Brontosaurus, not to mention the duck-billed Iguanodon, the armoured Stegosaurus, the horned Triceratops, and the fiercest of them all, the Dimetrodon."

"Jumpin' Jehoshaphat!" exclaimed Stumpy in openmouthed wonder. "Will you listen to the younker wrangle them words!"

Bartholomew B. Bartholomew cleared his throat. "Launcelot is something of a prodigy," he said, and if there was pardonable pride in his voice there was also a harassed look in his eye. "He wrote a treatise on the subject when he was seven years old."

"Oh, *that*," said Launcelot with a wave of his hand and a contemptuous toss of his yellow curls. "A very juvenile effort, *pater*. I've always felt a great deal prouder of my treatise which proved to my own satisfaction that the cycad forests of Tongaland were the Biblical Garden of Eden. But of course I was a year older, and my style was more mature."

Rowdy, not so sure now that Mark Champion had been smoking the wrong kind of weed, frowned. "You say your crews have been hitting the grit whenever they've seen these things?"

Champion sighed. "I'm using both Irish and Chinese in the grading and track-laying crews. But my labourers are predominantly Chinese. The Irish have merely sobered up at the sight of a Brontosaurus in the night, and then have proceeded to get drunk again as fast as possible. But the

Chinese have deserted in droves. Their mythology is dragon-studded, and they are convinced that they are seeing dragons.

"Dragon legends," said Launcelot, yawning widely, "undoubtedly stem from racial legends of the dinosaurs, and thus the myth persists among all peoples. You know, of course, that fossil remains of dinosaurs have been found in the rock of every continent."

Stumpy said firmly, "Thing to do is to chouse all the critters out of the canyons and corral them somewheres. Can't let 'em go interfering with the work."

Launcelot yawned again, patting his mouth delicately. "Dinosaurs," said he, "have been extinct for quite some time. Their sudden extinction has been attributed to various causes, but the theory that I favour is that they were unable to live in an increasingly cold climate. There were some violent disturbances, you know, in the Cretaceous period, which brought the Mesozoic to a close."

Stumpy, obviously to hide his bewilderment, nodded profoundly. "Seems I recollect some ruckuses of some sort, but I was pretty young at the time."

Launcelot regarded Stumpy with sudden interest. "Mr. Grampis," he said, "have you considered willing your skull to one of the museums?"

"Not till I'm through with it!" Stumpy retorted angrily.

Rowdy had been lost in thought. He was remembering that this was not the first reference to dinosaurs he'd heard since he'd come to the Weetigo country; the bland Doctor Quong had professed an interest in the extinct monsters. But Rowdy held that card close to his vest. "You spoke of other troubles," he said. "Human troubles. How about them?"

"McAllister can give you a full report when you get out to end-of-steel," Champion said. "We've run into many minor nuisances, some of them explainable, some of them not. They point to a definite attempt to slow us down. And our workers have been peppered by riflemen several times."

"Who's to gain if you don't get that spur through? Any other railroad interested?"

Champion shook his head. "It wouldn't pay them, since they'd have to build a main line. No, it can't be that. But the Chicago office may call off the whole job if I don't show sufficient progress. These delays cost money. I——"

He broke off in mid-sentence, for obviously, if the sounds were any indication, a tornado had got its tail in a wringer in the anteroom outside this conference room. There was confusion beyond the door, voices rising angrily and the bespectacled clerk wailing as though he'd got caught cross-wise in a stampede. Then Miss Arabella Hatter and her niece, Taisy, came storming through the doorway, the spinster with her bonnet askew and her blue eyes flashing angrily behind her steel-rimmed spectacles, the girl still bearing the bull whip and looking as though the ensuing hours since Rowdy had last seen her had done not one whit to improve her disposition.

"Miss Hatter!" Champion cried, coming to his feet again, but it was upon the girl that his eyes were fastened. "What is this?"

Miss Arabella shook a bony finger at the entire assemblage. "I'll tell you what it is," she cried shrilly. "It's a demand for action, young man. I'll have you know I'm a stockholder in the railroad you represent. If any young whipper-snapper thinks he can keep Arabella Hatter from stepping into an office that was probably furnished by the very money I invested, he's very much mistaken!"

Abner Grubb also rose to his feet, his long face softening with an ingratiating smile. "Won't you sit down," he urged. "You, too, Taisy. Now just what is the difficulty?"

"My spur," Miss Hatter snapped, still standing. "Or rather Cousin Lucius' spur. It was stolen, you know. But of course you don't know. I couldn't think of facing Cousin Lucius without fetching along the spur, since he made such

a point of my bringing it. And I have a right to demand
that the railroad throw its entire resources into finding the
spur."

She seemed to notice Rowdy and Stumpy for the first
time. "There are the scoundrels who stole it! Those two! I
wouldn't have believed it of them until my niece assured
me that they were once notorious outlaws! Mr. Smith, or
Dow, or whatever your name is, I insist that you return my
property."

"Cross my heart and hope to fall down and break both
my back legs," Rowdy said wearily. "I haven't got your
confounded spur."

Bartholomew cleared his throat impressively. "Would
you please be seated, ladies. I would like to have you co-
herently explain whatever is troubling you."

"You just split an infinitive, *pater*," said Launcelot.

"Quiet!" B.B. boomed, growing very red in the face.
"And now, ma'am——"

Miss Hatter controlled herself enough to tell the story
of the stagecoach trip, the attempted hold-up, and her dis-
covery afterwards that the spur was missing from her luggage.

"My niece quickly put two and two together when I
told her of the circumstances," she added. "But when she
accosted Mr. Dow or Mr. Smith, or whatever his name is,
he refused to give up the stolen property."

"Confound it," said Stumpy, "we couldn't fork over
what we didn't have!"

"I'm forced to reveal," said Mark Champion, "that
these men are employees of Montana Central. Their ruse
of travelling under assumed names was at the suggestion of
one of our officials. They come to us highly recommended.
If they say they haven't your spur, I'm sure they're telling
the truth."

"Very well," said Miss Hatter, somewhat calmed. "But
I must insist that the railroad come to my aid in recovering

the spur. Cousin Lucius will be furious when he learns I've lost it. As a stockholder——"

"Of course," Champion interjected hastily. "I pledge you that all of my organisations will lend an effort to recovering your property. Dow, you and Grampis keep that in mind. In fact, make it your main objective."

"Corsarn it——!" Stumpy began.

Miss Hatter smiled a benign smile. "I certainly couldn't ask for more co-operation than that, young man. Come, Taisy, these gentlemen probably have important business to discuss."

Taisy shifted herself; she had a feline grace to her, and she gave Rowdy Dow a long, smoky look. "I'm still not sure but what this buzzard has the spur," she said.

But she looked toward the door, her aunt with her; and Mark Champion, looking forlornly after Taisy, said, "I'm hoping to ride out your way, once I get caught up on my work."

"You do," said Taisy insolently, "and Mad Hatter's likely to dust your britches with a shotgun. You know how he feels about railroaders."

She closed the door behind her; and Champion stood staring for a long moment, looking like a man who'd been listening to the sweetest music in the world. Rowdy, as nettled as Stumpy but not showing it so plainly, said, "See here, Champion, I'm a man who can take orders, and I'm a sure enough trouble-shooter for the railroad right now. But damned if I can see myself beating the sagebrush for a lost spur!"

"Eh——?" Champion pulled himself from his reverie. "That may have been opportunity knocking loudly at our door, Dow. I had a notion when I pledged your help in finding that spur. Apparently Mad Hatter has some crazy reason for wanting it, and considering that Hatter is to say the least, slightly eccentric, humouring him might mean a very great deal to us. We want right-of-way across his range. If our finding that spur puts us in his good graces, it's worth the while. I'm giving you no specific orders, Dow. Your job is to help the railroad spur get through to Porphyry. But you might do well to keep your eye peeled for the spur the lady was speaking about."

Rowdy sighed. "We'll see what we can do about it. I think I'll head out to end-o'-steel and talk to this McAllister fellow. Me, I'd like to see those dinosaurs that walk by night."

"Me, too," said Stumpy.

Launcelot came around the table and tugged at Stumpy's chequered coat tail.

"I think it's only fair to tell you," said Launcelot, "that it's been some two hundred million years since dinosaurs were alive."

"That long?" said Stumpy, blinking.

Bartholomew got up from the table and paced to a window overlooking the street. Here he stood with his hands locked behind him, his feet spread apart, a man brooding upon great and imponderable things; and Launcelot said in a stage whisper that might have carried to the Weetigos, "Pretend you notice a resemblance to Napoleon. That always pleases the *pater*."

"Quiet!" B. B. boomed, growing redder in the face. "Launcelot, please remember that we're a long way from the restraining influence of your mother. I was raised to believe that to spare the rod is to spoil the child."

"Let the button go write a treaty about that!" Stumpy guffawed.

B. B. stood staring down into the street, then he beckoned the others to him. When they were grouped around the Easterner, Bartholomew said, "Look below. There you see the main street of a normal Montana town, busier than most, I'll concede, because a railroad has stirred it to life. But there is nothing here, gentlemen, that defies explanation; and I'm wondering if we all aren't letting ourselves get a little deluded. Dinosaurs! What nonsense! And even the more tangible troubles, such as you've reported to me,

Champion, are probably isolated vandalisms performed without thought or pattern. I simply find it impossible to subscribe to the theory that an organised effort is being made to stop a spur from being constructed to Porphyry."

"But our workers have been shot at!"

"Pooh, sir. Doubtless some cowboys having a little fun in their own uncouth way."

"That's the *pater,*" Launcelot observed. "Both feet on the solid ground."

Champion said slowly, "Maybe I've gotten jumpy lately."

"Of course you have, my boy," said B. B. with great joviality. "You've been working too hard, I dare say——"

But that was all Bartholomew B. Bartholomew was to dare say at the moment, for just then Rowdy Dow hurled a shoulder at him, sending the big man careening away from the window. At the same time, Rowdy shouted, "Down! Everybody!" For it was Rowdy who'd caught the glint of sunlight on a rifle barrel in the window of a saloon across the way. And it was Rowdy who'd moved, just as the rifle blasted, knocking the glass from the window before which the group had stood.

5   End-of-Steel

A man on his feet surveys the world from whatever position he has managed to attain, but, although the fact has been largely overlooked by students of applied democracy, a gunshot can be a great leveller. This was self-evident in Montana Central's conference room. For suddenly the group was levelled upon the floor, and all barriers of position and importance were levelled at the same time. Thus a railroad dignitary, a construction engineer, a cowtown banker, two trouble-shooters of doubtful antecedents, and a child prodigy were at once reduced to a common heap of squirming humanity, each motivated by a desire to keep his hide intact and to remove himself from danger as thoroughly as possible. They were like a milling beef herd with little Launcelot at the core of it, seriously outclassed in this aggregation of avoirdupois.

Rowdy was the first to pick himself from the floor, and he came to his feet with a gun in his hand. Keeping close to the wall, he peered from the window, watching for that telltale flash of sunlight upon a gun barrel across the way. He was quickly joined by Stumpy, who'd fished his forty-five from beneath his chequered coat and had the look of a man more than ready to do battle. Bartholomew B. Bartholomew was making wild, incoherent sounds and scrambling about on his hands and knees like a prize bull battling a bee. Mark Champion was endeavouring to put his own body between Launcelot and a second shot, and Abner Grubb cried shrilly: "It's an attack on my bank! That's what it is!"

"Shut up!" Rowdy ordered. "It's an attack on some-body's carcase."

"Chicago shall hear of this!" B. B. howled. "What did they think they were doing, sending a man out in this assassin-ridden land? I tell you, I'll make them appeal to the government for military aid. I'll have this state placed under martial law!"

"Easy, *pater*!" Launcelot cried warningly. "Remember what the doctor said about aggravating your asthma!"

No second shot came. Rowdy waited out a long moment and then darted across the conference room and into the ante-room, Stumpy at his heels. The bespectacled clerk, not fully recovered from his bout with the Misses Hatter, peered from behind his desk and said in a shaken voice, "Everything all right in there?"

"Right as rain," Rowdy assured him and went down the stairs to the street.

A gunshot in Tailholt had attracted no more attention than a raindrop in a reservoir; in the eternal roar of the boomtown the shot had been lost. Rowdy skipped across the street, dodging between freight wagons; and Stumpy toiled behind him, cursing the creators of yellow shoes and striving mightily to keep up. The two burst into the saloon from which the shot had come; and Rowdy looked around quickly, seeing the long bar with the apron behind it, seeing a few scattered tables and a few scattered patrons. The bartender fixed upon Rowdy a bored and disinterested look; and then the apron seemed to recall that he, himself, was here for more than decorative purposes.

"What'll it be?" that worthy demanded.

But Rowdy had already spied a stair at the back of the room, and to this he headed. Ascending with Stumpy close behind him, he found himself in a hall with doors giving from it. Rowdy had mentally marked the position of that room to the front of the building from which the shot had been fired, and he went unerringly to it and put his shoulder to the door and shoved hard, his gun in his hand again. He came lunging inside to find the room deserted.

An oilcloth-covered card table stood in the centre of the room, beneath an overhanging brass-bound lamp. A few chairs were strewn about, some of them overturned, and cards littered the floor, and in the atmosphere was a sweetish, cloying odour which Rowdy quickly identified. Opium had been smoked here. The room's one window was open, its dusty faded curtain flapping idly in the breeze. Rowdy edged to this window, and looking upward across the street, saw the window of the Odd Fellows building—the window before which the group had stood. Mark Champion was peering cautiously from the window, and Rowdy waved a reassuring hand at him. Then he looked down at the floor. An ejected rifle cartridge lay there.

"He cleared out fast," Stumpy muttered.

"We'll have a talk with the bartender," said Rowdy.

But when they came back down to the bar-room, the apron had little to offer. "Chinks rent that room," he explained when he was interrogated. "They use it for card games when they come to town from end-of-steel."

"Many of them up there this morning?"

The apron shrugged. "They come and they go. Sometimes they use the back door and slip upstairs. I don't pay no attention to 'em. What's eating you, mister?"

"Nothing a day in the country won't cure," said Rowdy. "You sure you didn't see one of them tote a rifle upstairs to-day?"

"Mister," said the barkeep, draping himself indolently against the bar, "I'm a busy man."

Outside, Rowdy paused on the boardwalk, lost in thought but alert enough, for he was remembering that the rifle-toting Celestial might still be within gunshot. "Doctor Quong again?" he mused aloud.

Stumpy said, "Which one of us do you reckon he was trying to get?"

"B. B., I'd judge," said Rowdy. "But maybe B. B. just

made the biggest target. Then again, the shot might have been to throw a scare into all of us. And it could have been any of a hundred Chinamen behind the gun. Yet they're not an aggressive people, and I can't figure any of the coolies doing gun work. That's why I keep thinking it was Quong. The trouble with education, Stumpy, is that it gives people too many ideas."

"We'd better go report to our bosses, Rowdy."

"Nothing much to report," said Rowdy. He was silent for a reflective moment. "Stumpy, we're going to split forces. Me, I'm going out to end-of-steel and talk to this Avalanche McAllister fellow. You stick around Tailholt."

Suspicion instantly seized Stumpy. "Confound it now, Rowdy," he said with considerable show of heat, "if you figger you're gonna corral all the fun——"

"There's a job to be done in Tailholt, old hoss," Rowdy said soothingly. "I want you to find Doctor Quong, if you can. He's got that spur, sure as shooting, and part of our job is to get it away from him. On top of that, somebody's got to be handy to play bodyguard for Bartholomew. Think what a blot it would be on our record if we both went out to end-of-steel and somebody punctured that big windbag while we were gone!"

Stumpy said, "Danged if I can see myself playing nursemaid to him!"

"Think how much smarter you'll be after associating with Launcelot for a while," Rowdy reminded him.

"I'll tear that button limb from limb," Stumpy threatened. His leathery face brightened. "You reckon I can quit being incognito, Rowdy?"

"Shouldn't wonder. Chances are that gent with the rifle was shooting at you to put you out of your misery. So long, Stumpy. I'll be seeing you soon. And I'll send for you pronto, if I run into anything too hard to handle."

"You take keer of yourself, Rowdy," his partner admonished him. "Don't you go taking no 'dobe dollars."

Whereupon Rowdy cut across town to the railroad

tracks, making the last lap on the run, for a work train was just chugging out of Tailholt, its clanging bell manifesting its impatience, its whistle warning the laggards. Rowdy swung aboard and found a seat for himself in a car crowded with graders and track-layers of two races. There were vociferous Irishmen, sun-reddened fellows wearing high boots with pantaloons tucked in the legs, and flannel shirts with no tie except a black handkerchief. Most of these men were nursing epic hangovers. A scattering of Chinese were in the car, keeping in a silent huddle and peering from the windows with bland and seemingly disinterested eyes.

Rowdy hunched down unobtrusively and lost himself in thought; the train gave a lurch. There was this one coach and a few flatcars loaded with rails and ties, the whole requiring some mighty heaving on the part of the engine. The train put Tailholt behind and jolted over the unballasted road-bed towards it destination.

Beyond the town, the country lay flat and monotonous and sage-studded, much the same sort of terrain as that over which Rowdy had rolled in the stagecoach the day before. But always the Weetigos were looming nearer, and Rowdy saw that thunderheads were gathering about those distant peaks. At times the track paralleled that ancient unused road which had brought Rowdy and his partner into Tailholt, and he wondered if Miss Arabella Hatter and her niece were travelling the road, heading to the Hatter ranch. Rowdy sighed. Quite a gal, that Taisy.

After the first few miles, the country began to undergo a change, becoming broken and rocky, and the track spanned a ravine over a high, spider-legged trestle. Soon they were into canyons, a country of towering white walls and long drops, and the track, which had run straight as an arrow out of Tailholt began winding sinuously, following the meanderings of a canyon. Rowdy saw the dark mouths of other canyons emptying into this big one. A weird and forlorn land, the canyon country, and Rowdy unconsciously shuddered, remembering the dinosaurs. A man might see anything in this misshapen world.

Only a few hours out of Tailholt, they came to end-of-steel, and Rowdy sat bolt upright. This far the spur had reached and no farther; and here, where the canyon was broadest, weatherbeaten tents, grey and tattered, flapped in the breeze; and construction shacks were strewn about, and supplies were heaped everywhere. Workers swarmed aimless as ants; loose ties were piled high, and sledges clanged ceaselessly. The bridge crews were up ahead, possibly a tunnel crew was even farther beyond, at Humpback Hill, but here the graders and track-layers toiled while engines funnelled black smoke against the sky, and the rails moved forward to the steady commands of "Up! Forward! Ready! Down!" Sledges clanged, and the spur moved twenty-eight feet nearer Porphyry. Teamsters hurled blistering invective upon horses, adding to the wild confusion.

Swinging down from the work train, Rowdy headed for a shack where a telegraph instrument made its constant chatter, and voicing an inquiry, was directed to a special car standing on a siding. This was the office of the officials, and here he would find Avalanche McAllister. Rowdy climbed aboard the car and thereupon confronted the largest man he had ever seen.

"Weel, mon," said Avalanche McAllister with a scowl that would have intimidated the huskiest terrier, "what are ye standing there for?"

The man was seated behind a desk, glaring at a litter of official-looking papers as though he'd like to have blown them away with a whoosh of his breath, and there was a burr to McAllister's speech upon which a man could have pegged his sombrero. For McAllister in direct violation to the legend that all railroad construction bosses must be Irish, was a Scot, a huge red-faced sandy-haired giant with whiskers that might have stood currying. Muscled and wind-burned, he was a considerable hunk of man, and

Rowdy judged that an explosive temper lay buried none too deeply beneath that rocky exterior.

"I'm Rowdy Dow," said Rowdy. "Mark Champion just put me on the payroll. Trouble-shooter. What's holding up this spur?"

McAllister's scowl grew blacker. "Tr-rouble, lad! Big tr-rouble, ye ken. 'Tis everything that's going wr-rong, and them beasties in the night is the wor-rst of it. Somebody doesn't want this spur to go through. 'Tis wearing me to a shadow, the wor-ryin' and the grievin'."

Rowdy said, "Anything special that I can start chipping away at?"

"This mon, Hatter," said Avalanche McAllister. "Our grading-crews are a'most to the bor-rders of his ranch. 'Tis guns he's going to greet us with. Ye might try talking a wee bit o' sense to the mon."

"I've met some of the family," Rowdy said dryly. "They have a language of their own."

"Ah," said McAllister, brightening. " 'Tis the lassie that's caught your eye!" He frowned again. "A wee kiss I tried to steal from her, do ye ken, and she belted me with her whup something fierce. Go to Hatter's, if ye wish, lad. But it's na me that's envying ye the job."

Rowdy said, "Got a spare horse around these parts? Seems I've got to the end of the line."

"Ye'll find saddle stock along with the wor-rk stock, lad. Help yourself. I like your cut, mon. We'll get along fine."

Rowdy extended his hand. "This is a new game to me," he confessed. "But if we've got to put a railroad through, we've got to put a railroad through. I'll keep in touch with you, McAllister. If anything busts loose, let me know. I shouldn't be at Hatter's long."

"Guid luck to ye, lad," said McAllister, and, taking Rowdy's extended hand, proceeded to numb the knuckles.

A man appeared in the doorway of the private car, a shirt-sleeved man with a green visor, whom Rowdy instantly recognised as the telegrapher who had directed him here. But now this man gave Rowdy a look that held more than ordinary interest and said guardedly, "Telegram for you, chief. Just came." He extended a flimsy yellow sheet to McAllister.

"An order to hurry the tr-rack laying, I'll war-rant ye," said McAllister. He took the message and read it, his sandy eyebrows bunching and his beard seeming to grow stiffer, and suddenly he turned, his huge hand falling upon Rowdy's shoulder, and he lifted Rowdy from the floor of the car and shook him. The terrible temper which Rowdy had guessed had now burst through the surface, and the voice of Avalanche McAllister was a roar in his ears.

"Ye skellum, ye!" McAllister shouted. "So ye'd pull the wool over the eyes of Angus McAllister, eh!" He shook Rowdy harder. " 'Tis every bone in your body I'll break!"

Rowdy managed to shout, "What is this?"

McAllister thrust the telegram under Rowdy's nose, and Rowdy glimpsed these dancing words:

BE ON LOOKOUT FOR MAN CALLING HIMSELF ROWDY DOW WHO WILL CLAIM TO BE TROUBLE-SHOOTER HIRED BY ME. FELLOW IS IMPOSTER OBVIOUSLY OUT TO MAKE TROUBLE FOR RAILROAD. HANDLE HIM AS YOU SEE FIT.

And to this was appended the name of Mark Champion.

Staring with disbelieving eyes, Rowdy grasped hard at one thought: he was glad he'd left Stumpy behind in Tailholt, for something almighty wrong was brewing there, and this telegram was the proof of it. But he had no way of giving the lie to the telegram, not with red wrath boiling in McAllister and the man's heavy hand upon him.

6 ⋮ That Sleuth Stumpy

Stumpy Grampis, that frontier fashion plate, had with mingled emotions watched Rowdy take leave of him in Tailholt and head for the work train and end-of-steel, for past experience had taught Stumpy that when the work was divided it was usually Rowdy who fell heir to the real excitement. By grab, Fate could be as crooked as a warped corkscrew! For Stumpy, while often pretending a great ardour for the peaceful paths, actually craved to be in the thick of epic events. Confound it, it weren't right that when excitement was apt to be whizzing by, a man should be side-tracked with a busted axle. It left Stumpy three-thirds disgusted.

Therefore he stood upon the boardwalk across from the Odd Fellows building and regarded Tailholt's teeming street with an exceedingly jaundiced and unenthusiastic eye. Then bestirring himself to a show of activity, he crossed over and climbed the stairs to the railroad offices where he found the three men and the boy awaiting him.

"Come to report," said Stumpy and told of his and Rowdy's fruitless search of the room over the saloon. "Rowdy's gone on to end-o'-steel," he concluded. "Me, I've got my work cut out. Gotta find that ding-blasted spur. And I aim to see that no harm comes to you folks whilst Rowdy is frying other fish."

Little Launcelot looked impressed. "You mean you're to be our bodyguard?"

"That's the idea, younker."

"Ha! Ha! Ha!" laughed Launcelot.

"Now see here——!" Stumpy began, a dangerous

glint in his eye; but Launcelot suddenly sobered, taking on a look of cherubic innocence that somehow reminded Stumpy of Rowdy when Rowdy was getting ready to pull a whizzer on him. "I'll help you find the spur," said Launcelot.

"Don't need no help," Stumpy mumbled ungraciously. "That there chore I'll do with my *left* hand."

"The whole thing revolves around a simple problem of deduction," Launcelot went on relentlessly. "The spur obviously has a value, in spite of its seeming worthlessness. This Doctor Quong, who was aboard the stage, must have laid hands on it. That we can safely assume by applying the process of elimination. What will Quong do with it now that he has it? Why, he'll keep it close to his person, since —as we have agreed—it is a thing of value. Ergo, find Doctor Quong and you have found the spur."

"That's exactly the way I figured it," said Stumpy, who in strict honesty had done no such thing.

Mark Champion stirred himself. "Got to get to work," he announced. "There are at least a dozen wires to be sent to the construction camp."

"I should be getting down to the bank," said Abner Grubb. He regarded Stumpy with the shadow of a frown. "I presume Dow knew what he was doing when he left you here alone."

Stumpy bristled, fighting mightily against an urge to tweak the banker's long nose. "Me, I'm the *senior* partner of the firm," he insisted. "When occasion calls for judicious judgment, I'm the galoot who's elected to handle the reins."

"Ha! Ha! Ha!" crowed Launcelot.

Stumpy turned toward the door, an itch in the palm of his hand that demanded he apply said palm to the posterior of little Launcelot, and he had to struggle against this desire. Moreover, Abner Grubb hadn't made Stumpy's day any brighter, but at the door, Stumpy got in a parting thrust. "You gents better stay behind walls," he said.

"Can't be with you all of the time, and you ain't likely safe unless I'm around."

"Ha! Ha! Ha!" said Launcelot.

Muttering to himself, Stumpy came down to the street and again stood gazing at Tailholt, feeling as futile as a woodpecker with a busted beak. Across the way was the saloon he and Rowdy had visited, and Stumpy was suddenly reminded that he had craved a drink last night and forgotten to get it. By grab, he could go and have one now! A man was entitled to a little bolstering when he had work to do that made the chores of that feller Hercules seem like something to be handled in an off hour. Yet, although temptation tugged mightily at Stumpy's chequered coat tail, wisdom dictated that he keep away from the fire-water.

No, sir, he couldn't be drinking till the work was done. That bit of wisdom had been handed to Stumpy by his dear departed father, and there was no gainsaying that Grampis Senior had been an authority. Hadn't the old man, at the very time he'd spoken on the subject, been earning a reasonably honest dollar by sitting on the platform of a temperance lecturer who made his speech more emphatic by pointing out Stumpy's dad as the horrible example of what came of jousting with the Demon Rum? Stumpy sighed. The old man had been something of a celebrity at that stage of his career, but the job hadn't paid off. The temperance lecturer always drank up the profits.

Sighing again, Stumpy resolutely looked away from the saloon and fell to studying the passers-by. They were a motley assortment—townsmen, spur-jangling cowboys from the ranches, bearded construction workers, miners down from Porphyry, a few Chinese. Most of the Celestials wore the rough garb of graders or track-layers, and nowhere was to be seen the dapper, well-tailored figure of the elusive Doctor Quong.

By grab, a man would have to do some sleuthing to catch up with Quong, but Stumpy did not consider himself inadequately trained for the task. Hadn't he, in his day, perused a vast number of paper-backed novels pertaining to the adventures of various fictional sleuths who invariably got their man? These human bloodhounds, Stumpy recalled, had relied heavily upon disguise, but Stumpy, in that sense, was already prepared. He was disguised in a chequered suit.

Whereupon Stumpy was suddenly struck with a thought so startling as to take the wind out of him. Suppose Doctor Quong had changed from his black suit of Occidental cut to the garb of a working coolie? Confound it, looking for him would then be like looking for a hatpin in a haystack! Now Stumpy numbered a few Chinese among his friends, notably a certain Hop Gow of Helena who was ostensibly a dealer in jade and tea but who smuggled his countrymen across the border in the dark of the moon as a lucrative sideline. Stumpy would have recognised Hop Gow's rotund figure in a high fog; but like most of his own race, Stumpy saw Chinese as looking more or less alike. He tried recalling whether Quong had worn a pigtail, but he couldn't be sure. Possibly it had been coiled beneath his hat.

Peering hard at such Chinese as passed, Stumpy shortly began to see Doctor Quong in each and every one of them. Those bland smiles—those slanted eyes. It was as irritating as trying to pick a fly out of a pepper shaker, and Stumpy's anger grew until out of pure frustration he seized the wrist of the next Oriental who came along.

"Over here!" Stumpy ordered fiercely and dragged the stunned Celestial into a weedy slot between two buildings. Quickly Stumpy ran his hands over the loose garb of his captive, feeling for the hard outlines of a hidden spur; and the coolie, at first petrified with fright, began squawking and struggling like a captured chicken. He tried tearing free of Stumpy, and his shirt was wrenched open in the process. Stumpy caught a glimpse of a yellow, hairless chest, crossed by a white scar that had undoubtedly been acquired through active participation in tong politics. Then the man broke free and bolted.

Stumpy let him go, satisfied that this one carried no hidden spur. But Stumpy's anger was still prodding him. Shucks, a man couldn't expect to find the spur on the first Chinaman who came along! That would be busting the law of averages so badly they'd likely put him in jail.

Lying in wait, he waylaid a second Chinese, and again he drew a blank. A third and fourth were also spurless, and one of them put up a fairly stiff fight. Stumpy was now warming to his work, and he was putting a high polish to it. Instead of standing on the boardwalk from which he then had to drag the Chinese, to the raucous amusement of passing cowboys, he took to staying around a corner of a building and darting out to pounce upon a new candidate. This strategy netted him his fifth and sixth captives, and again he made his search, and again he had a struggle on his hands. Number six's shirt got torn open, and there, upon the fellow's yellow, hairless chest was the white scar. Stumpy let the man go.

Confound it, man number six had likewise been man number one. A plague on a race that looked all alike!

Whereupon Stumpy, visualising himself endlessly searching the same Chinaman over and over, grew fit to be tied. He couldn't keep duplicating the work, and he couldn't go throwing a brand on each coolie he examined, thereby precluding the possibility of examining that same one again. First place, he had no branding iron, and in the second place there was probably a law agin it. He had a good notion to go and get himself a drink. Several drinks! He wandered back to the boardwalk and spied a mercantile store up the street. Suppose he got a can of paint and a brush and put a mark on each Chinese he inspected? The idea seemed both sound and futile. Stumpy dropped the whole fruitless project.

There was no longer any need to be travelling incognito, and he bethought himself to get out of his outlandish garb. By grab, he had some *human* duds in his carpetbag, and maybe a man could think clearer if he was dressed properly. Bowlegging to the Traveller's Rest, Stumpy found the same desk clerk on duty who had greeted him so affably last night, inquiring into his line of goods.

"How's business?" the clerk asked.

"Plumb ruint," said Stumpy and climbed the stairs. In the upper hall he almost stumbled over an all-too-familiar figure which he instantly regarded with unveiled suspicion. "What you doing here?" he demanded of little Launcelot Bartholomew.

"Why, we have quarters here, the *pater* and I," said Launcelot in a mild and disarming voice. "Didn't you know?"

"No, I didn't," said Stumpy sourly. "Git out of my way, or I'll trample you under."

"I'm sorry if I startled you, Mr. Grampis," said Launcelot in the same mild voice.

Stumpy stumbled past the boy and let himself into the room he and Rowdy had shared. Shooting up the blind, he regarded the unmade bed and also regarded his carpetbag. His cue was to get into other clothes and get back about his sleuthing; but the bed, even in its dishevelled state, looked mighty inviting. By grab, it surely made sense that a man couldn't do his best thinking when he was plumb tuckered out; and it likewise followed, as surely as sparrows followed horses, that a bit of rest would sharpen the edge of a fellow's capabilities.

Having with no great effort sold himself on this faultless bit of logic, Stumpy divested himself of the hated yellow shoes, peeled out of his drummer duds and stood in the long-handled underwear which he wore at all seasons. Thus garbed, he flopped down upon the bed. And immediately rose a good three feet into the air, at the same time letting out a yowl that shook the rafters of the ancient edifice.

Lighting on the floor, he pulled himself to a stand and

tugged away the blanket upon which he'd presumed to rest. Beneath it were spurs—at least a dozen of them—and upon these many rowels Stumpy had roosted so briefly. And while he stood staring, the eldritch laughter of little Launcelot floated down the hall and percolated through the flimsy door.

A red and murderous rage upon him, Stumpy got to the door in a single bound and was off down the hall as fast as his legs could carry him. Launcelot, apparently unprepared for the swiftness of Stumpy's coming, bolted ahead of him; but Stumpy, reaching out, got a good hold in those dancing yellow curls. Launcelot's howl of anguish brought open a nearby door—the door that Launcelot had been trying to attain—and the doorway was filled by the huge figure of Bartholomew B. Bartholomew.

"What is this?" B. B. demanded.

"Spurs!" Stumpy spluttered. "He filled my bed with spurs!"

"I was only trying to be of help," Launcelot shrieked. "I told him I'd assist him in finding the spur. The man has no sense of appreciation! It took me a long time to gather those spurs. Most of them I had to remove from the boots of inebriated cowboys who were sleeping behind saloons."

B. B. cleared his throat uneasily. "Perhaps the boy was really trying to be of service."

"But he put 'em in my bed!" Stumpy howled.

"If one of them was the valuable spur, I didn't want it left around in plain sight," Launcelot argued, having regained his usual composure. "As it was, I was very careful to get the key to your room without even the desk clerk seeing me, and to restore it afterwards."

"Blast it——!" Stumpy raged, and raised his hand.

"Ahem," said Bartholomew B. Bartholomew uneasily. "I suggest you give the boy the benefit of the doubt, Grampis. Naturally his mother—er—holds me personally responsible for his welfare while on this trip."

Stumpy's hand dropped and he reluctantly released

his hold on Launcelot, for in the eyes of Bartholomew Senior there was a mute appeal that would have softened stone, and suddenly Stumpy felt a kinship to the big man. It was as though they both had the same cross to bear. Aware now that he was standing here in the hallway of the hotel in his underwear, while people, aroused by the ruckus, were opening doors and peering out, Stumpy wordlessly turned and headed back towards his own room. It had been, he reflected ruefully, a most difficult day.

7 ⋮ Betwixt and Between

Now Rowdy Dow, like his bedevilled partner Stumpy, was also having a difficult day. No man in his right senses will endeavour to argue with an avalanche, and Rowdy was beginning to understand how Montana Central's construction boss had come by this soubriquet. This Avalanche McAllister had all the power of a rock pile cavorting down a mountainside, and he made just about as much noise. Moreover, Rowdy, dangling in the man's grip and being shaken until his teeth rattled, was in no position to voice a defence. But at last McAllister ceased dancing Rowdy, though he still kept a firm grip on him.

"Look!" Rowdy shouted. "That telegram's a fake! You check with Champion and you'll find that out!"

Anger still glinted in McAllister's eyes. "Mon, do ye think ye can deceive me twict? Daft I'd be to call my better a liar!"

"Just the same, you check!"

McAllister hurled the dizzy Rowdy into the arms of the telegrapher who was astute enough to pluck Rowdy's gun at once from its holster. "Champion will be out to end-o'-steel to-night, mon," McAllister growled. " 'Tis then he can see you. Lock him up now, till the boss comes drappin' by."

The telegrapher prodded Rowdy with his own gun. "Move along, you!" he ordered.

Rowdy shrugged in surrender. Logic couldn't stop an avalanche, and neither could a show of strength, especially when Rowdy had just been stripped of his armament. He allowed himself to be conducted from the car and along the siding to a tool shed. Into this he was thrust, and the door was padlocked. Rowdy rearranged his dishevelled clothes and seated himself upon something which proved to be a powder keg and stared about in the gloom. A fine howdy-you-do this was!

He could merely sit here until Mark Champion arrived that night, whereupon he would be released. That telegram was a mistake—worse than that, it was a deliberate effort to discredit him. But who had made such a play? He thought of Bartholomew B. Bartholomew and Abner Grubb; both of them had been reluctant to see him and Stumpy placed upon Montana Central's payroll. Yet B. B. could have overruled Champion this morning if he'd wished, and Grubb had pledged cooperation once Mark Champion had taken a strong stand on behalf of the trouble-shooters. He thought of Doctor Quong. But would Quong have had access to the railroad's telegraph?

This speculating was a fruitless occupation, and with his eyes growing accustomed to the darkness, Rowdy saw that the shack was littered with all sorts of tools—shovels, sledges, picks, crowbars—and there were kegs of spikes and kegs of powder and coils of fuse. With all these things at hand it would require little effort to force his way out of this shack; in fact, he'd never seen a prison so well supplied with the implements of escape. But why escape, since he'd be free anyway when Champion arrived?

Still, his restive soul rebelled at this confinement; besides, he had work to do. Not pressing work exactly, but a man certainly wasn't earning his salt sitting on his posterior on a powder keg. Coming to a stand, Rowdy plucked a crowbar from a corner and gently inserted its end between door and frame and began to exert pressure. The padlock hasp groaned and threatened to part from the screws which held it.

Instantly Rowdy was arrested by a voice so thick with Irish brogue that a man couldn't have poked his finger through it. "Yez kape that up, me bhoy," said the voice, "and I'll be coming in there to bend a sledge handle over yer skull!"

They'd posted a guard, of course. With a sigh, Rowdy restored the crowbar to its corner and seated himself upon the powder keg again. He would, it appeared, be staying here until he gazed upon the sunburned face of Mark Champion.

Twiddling his thumbs for a while, he resigned himself to his predicament. Beyond the shack all the roar of construction rose, and he tried sorting out the sounds, one from another, and identifying them. He could hear the rumbling of freight wagons and the steady clanging of a locomotive's bell and the ring of sledges. At a distance he made out another sound, a faint rumbling, and he guessed that some blasting was being done in these canyons. When the sound repeated itself, he decided it was thunder, and he remembered the clouds he'd seen gathering around the peaks of the Weetigos earlier in the day.

It grew oppressively sultry in this tiny shack, and time seemed to drag endlessly, and there was no way to gauge it. The shack was without windows, and only a little light showed around the edges of the door and between the planking. He could tell when dusk began to gather, but he was sure that at least three years passed before the light faded. Thereafter the door was opened and a brawny track-layer with the map of Ireland stamped upon his face presented him with a bucket of stew.

"Eat it, me bhoy," said this son of Erin. " 'Twill put hair on your chist."

Rowdy fell to eating, glad of the diversion. "Champion showed up yet?" he asked.

The Irishman frowned. "If he has, he ain't reported to Paddy O'Rourke, seeing as that's niver been his custom. Go on with ye, bhoy. What would Champion want with the loikes of ye?"

"I'm teaching him how to braid a reata," said Rowdy. "He always drops in every night for a lesson."

"A reata, is it? A rope, ye mean! And when ye get it finished, maybe we'll put it around your neck and hang ye. 'Tis spalpeens like yez that has made life a misery for us, a-working on the railroad."

Remembering what Mark Champion and Avalanche McAllister had both hinted about the troubles that beset the building of this spur, Rowdy knew what the man meant. An impostor, such as Rowdy appeared to be, might very well be one of the breed who had harassed the construction crews in sundry ways. Still, Rowdy was only faintly alarmed.

"Look like rain?" he asked.

The Irishman shuddered. "The thunder's moving closer."

"Well," said Rowdy, "it won't bite you. You can take this bucket and your face out of here."

Soon the door was closed and locked behind his departing guard, but Rowdy could hear the restless movements of the man beyond the flimsy wall, and now there was nothing for Rowdy to do but return to his eternal waiting. The darkness closed down upon the canyons and it was like the inside of a stovepipe in the shack, and the thunder continued its muttering and a few drops of rain spattered upon the shack's roof. And still Champion failed to put in an appearance.

It was, Rowdy reflected dismally, going to be a long, dull night. He wondered how Stumpy was faring.

And then all hell broke loose.

The day's work was done, but still this construction camp was one vast cauldron of sound, men making talk around supper fires and tools being stacked and switch engines at their everlasting chuffing and panting. Among all these sounds, Rowdy was slow to recognise the new note, and then it was there—the drumming of hoofs, faint at first but growing louder and louder upon the rocky floor of the canyon. The rain was coming down harder, the thunder speaking oftener; but now guns were making their thunder, too, and voices rose, shrill with fright—the voices of the Chinese coolies. And suddenly pandemonium was upon the camp.

This was a raid. And Rowdy, realising the fact, was instantly to the door and pounding upon it. "Let me out!" he shouted, but he drew no response from the guard. A bullet splintered the door only a few inches above Rowdy's head; hoofs beat beyond—a raider had fired a random shot and galloped past. Rowdy judged that the guard had bolted. Dashing to the corner, Rowdy fumbled for a crowbar and got it between door and frame, and this time there was no opposition. The hasp snapped, and Rowdy burst from the shack.

Around him was chaos gone crazy. At least a score of raiders had struck the camp; and these men, mounted, were everywhere, firing wildly and sending the construction workers scurrying. Somewhere a shack blazed in the night, the fire roaring hungrily in spite of the rain, and by this light and that of the supper fires, Rowdy saw horsemen spreading terror. One wheeled by him, the rider hauling back on his reins and striking with his gun-barrel at an Irishman who gave him fight, wielding a pick-handle. The Irishman went down, and the raider roared onward, but Rowdy had had that glimpse of him.

And Rowdy knew the man. There was something about his bulk or the way he sat his saddle that identified him. He was one of the three who had stopped a stagecoach on the other side of Tailholt the day before. He was the one who had come to the coach and demanded of Miss Arabella Hatter that she surrender the spur she was carrying.

He was one of the three Doctor Quong had signalled with a wave of a white handkerchief.

And now Rowdy found himself in the same predicament as had the Irishman who'd just gone down beneath a swung gun-barrel. Another raider came roaring along and leaned from his saddle to strike at Rowdy. Grasping at the man's gun arm, Rowdy pulled, hauling the man from his horse, and the two of them went down in a heap. Fighting hard, Rowdy got the man beneath him and wrested the gun from him; and when the man got a grip on Rowdy's throat and squeezed hard, Rowdy struck at him blindly with the man's own gun. The man went limp beneath him, and Rowdy climbed to his feet, the gun in his hand.

The man's horse had got itself tangled in a fallen tent, and Rowdy rushed to the horse and snatched at its reins and was quickly into the saddle. Now he had a horse beneath him and a gun against his palm, and he felt ready to tackle the world and any satellite planets that wanted to buy into the fight. But when he looked around him, he saw that the raiders, their attack completed, were turning tail and heading west. Apparently this was their strategy: to dash in and wreak as much havoc as possible and dash away again. And Rowdy was at once after them. He wanted to know where these men nested, and he meant to find out.

The rain was pelting down harder, soaking Rowdy to the skin; and beneath that downpour, the fires the raiders had set were sizzling out, and darkness blanketed the camp. But the lightning moved across the black sky, making the scene day-bright and unearthly, and hard on the heels of the lightning the thunder roared, echoing and re-echoing in the canyons; and the voice of Avalanche McAllister outroared the thunder. For McAllister was here, and in the lightning flash Rowdy saw him waving a fist, and men came swarming towards Rowdy.

He got the horse to going, wishing mightily that he had spurs, and he sensed what was in the mind of McAllister. The gigantic construction boss presumed that this raid had been for the purpose of freeing Rowdy, and thus Rowdy was now doubly damned. But Rowdy had a horse under him and a skill at handling a cayuse, and he wheeled in the darkness and was off. He took the trail of the raiders, realising fully that this move would only convince McAllister the more that he was a member of that wild-riding crew. Yet if he had to make a run, Rowdy reasoned that he might as well be following his first plan of trailing the raiders.

The lightning came again, and Rowdy tried to memorise the camp in that brief moment of illumination. Also he tried to catch a glimpse of the departing raiders, and he saw them up ahead, single-filing into a canyon that gave into this one. Tangled tents and piled tools and shacks made multiple hazards; but Rowdy had got his glimpse of the terrain, and he urged his horse recklessly, risking disaster. For upon him the Irish and the Chinese were swarming and it was get out or get caught. He had his bad moments before he was free of the camp; twice the horse stumbled and almost pitched him from the saddle, and then he was beyond the last impedimenta, but still the construction crews howled at his heels.

Rowdy raised the horse to a good stiff gallop and kept it at that pace for several minutes. Then he reined short, listening intently in the downpour and waiting for the lightning to flare again. It seemed forever before the skies were riven, and then he saw what he was looking for—the canyon mouth into which the raiders had disappeared. But he also saw the workers swarming over the canyon floor from their devastated camp. He gave the horse a taste of his heels and sent the cayuse into the canyon he'd glimpsed.

Here was a fine case of being betwixt and between! Ahead were the raiders, and he wanted to trail them to their hide-out, but he couldn't crowd them too closely. Not without risking being recognised in a lightning flash. Yet if he loitered in order to keep distance between himself and those he was following, he was apt to fall into the hands of the vengeance-thirsty construction crew. He could hear the throaty cursing of the Irish, the shrill raucousness of the Chinese, the sounds beating steadily in the night. But now he was into the canyon. The question was whether the lightning had revealed him to those who were in pursuit.

Within a very few minutes he had his answer. The graders and track-layers were also in this canyon, swarming over its floor, fanning out and calling to one another in the sleazy dark. Rowdy's urge was to lift the horse again to a gallop, but this was far too risky. Boulders littered the floor of this canyon, which was much narrower than the one in which the track was being laid, and to hurry was to court disaster. He'd taken too many risks of that sort to-night; and Lady Luck, that fickle jade, couldn't be expected to have her arms around a fellow forever.

Yet as he picked his way along, he was gnawed by the certainty that those on foot were drawing closer to him. He could hear them not far behind, and it seemed that some were to his left and some to his right; and when the lightning came again, he saw movement so close by that he might have leaned from his saddle and touched a man. This fellow who had succeeded in outdistancing all the others was one of the Chinese, and he posed a problem. Rowdy had no desire to do the man harm, but the coolie was under no such restriction. He carried a pick-handle, and he swung it at Rowdy with considerable gusto. But the blow fell short.

And then so many things happened at once that Rowdy was afterwards sore put to sort out the events in anything approximating a proper sequence. There was the lightning, flaring again, and the Chinaman moving in to take a second and more favourable swipe with the pick-handle, and a dozen others like him converging to drag Rowdy from the horse. There was the pelting rain, and the canyon walls looming on either side, and the boulder-littered floor. There was noise and confusion and all the world bathed briefly in a chalky glow. And there was that huge ghostly thing moving just yonder, moving in the downpour and looking like nothing Rowdy had ever seen before, because this was his first look at a dinosaur. He only knew that he was beholding something out of another age, something escaped from a nightmare.

And then the darkness closed down, and in the drenched gloom the voices of the Chinese rose, shrill with terror; and the coolies were stampeding in panic, heading back towards their camp. And Rowdy's horse, which seemed to share the Chinese horror of dragons, was also bolting—but in its blind panic it was heading straight to where that huge thing lumbered in the night!

8 : Hatter's Place

In Rowdy now was a feeling of unearthly weirdness that left him more shaken than had the hand of Avalanche McAllister. From the first, Rowdy had scoffed at the notion that Mark Champion's construction crews might actually be harassed by dinosaurs, for Rowdy was a practical man with a touch of the Missourian in him. He had to be shown. He knew little of dinosaurs—he'd seen pictures of them in magazines which had fallen into his hands, and he understood vaguely that they had been extinct for countless centuries, and he would have placed his betting money that possibly they had never existed at all. Palaeontology was just a jaw-breaking word to him, but to-night he had seen a dinosaur.

Moreover, his fear-stricken horse was bolting blindly and apt to career into that monster so briefly glimpsed in the lightning's flare, and Rowdy was suddenly afraid— more afraid than he'd ever been in his hectic life—and unashamed of his fear. It was made of something primitive and uncontrollable and it brought the short hairs rising at the nape of his neck, and he had the feeling of moving through a nightmare. He found himself clutching at the saddlehorn, like the merest novice at riding. He found himself wishing heartily that he would awake to find Stumpy snoring at his side.

The lightning came again. Rowdy glimpsed the canyon walls and nothing more; the darkness descended, and thunder hammered at his ears; and the horse plunged wildly through blackness and noise, stumbling often on the rocky underfooting. He let the horse run; he was not even certain which direction they were heading, and he found only one thing of which to be glad; the Chinese had been routed. Rowdy had the dinosaur to thank for that. Those workers, urged onward by the roaring voice of Avalanche McAllister and by anger at the recent raid, might have torn Rowdy to pieces if they'd laid hands on him. In their minds he was most definitely a partner to the men who'd stormed the camp.

Rowdy moved blindly through the night and the rain until at last the horse spent itself and Rowdy's fear spent itself, and the jaded mount plodded onward with Rowdy soaked in the saddle and having nothing to do but aimlessly go wherever the horse took him. He sensed that they had quitted the canyon where the dinosaur had made its appearance, and he had long since given up any hope of trailing the raiders. But he had this thought: the horse had belonged to one of that crew and perhaps the horse might instinctively head to their hideout.

As a trouble-shooter, Rowdy reflected, he needed another trouble-shooter to shoot his own troubles.

An hour passed and another and the rain slackened and finally died away to a mere drizzle, and at long last a feeble moon fought its way through the blanketing clouds and took a peep at the canyon country. Rowdy, now thoroughly lost, could only recognise that he was heading in a general north-westerly direction. Tired and wet, he longed for the morning; and by the time the moon had faded, he was too weary to go on. Still, he pushed forward for a while and then stopped, dragged the saddle from the horse and spread the blanket upon the ground. He found a gunny sack tied behind the saddle and he used this to squaw-hobble the horse. Then he laid down, pillowing his head upon the saddle. He had most uncomfortable bedding, but he soon fell asleep.

The sun, beating against his eyes, awoke him, and his first consciousness was that the horse had gone; it had slipped the hobble in the night. Frowning, Rowdy wished that he possessed Stumpy's sulphuric vocabulary, but he did his best with what words he knew. He'd wanted that horse; he had no desire to be left afoot in this tangle of canyons, and, besides, the horse might have led him to the raiders' hide-out. But if there was no sense in crying over spilled milk, it likewise followed that nothing was to be gained by wailing over a wilful cayuse.

Rowdy was both hungry and thirsty, but he was able to ease the one need, for rain-water had collected in pockets in the rocks. He was in another of those innumerable canyons, and it was mid-morning, and he was alone in the lost world. Far away came the dim sound of a locomotive's whistle, and as he listened he judged that the construction camp was many miles to the south-east, though he couldn't be sure of either the direction or the distance. He thought of the dinosaur; the monster of the night seemed like something he had dreamed. Hoisting the saddle and hooking it over his right hip, he began trudging along the canyon. And in due course he came to its end and climbed a ridge and found before him a spread of country that stretched to the eye's limit.

Here was terrain different from the endless sage flats that lay to the east of Tailholt and different too from the broken land of canyons which Rowdy had traversed by night. Ahead spread a tawny land of lush graze, broken by intermittent clumps of trees, the whole lying before the mighty back-drop of the Weetigos. Nearer a huge hill reared itself almost due west of where Rowdy stood. Between here and the hill, ranch buildings sprawled, smoke rising lazily from the chimney of one; and suddenly Rowdy realised where he was. He was remembering the map Mark Champion had showed him in Tailholt. He had crossed the canyon country, and beyond him lay Hatter's place, and that huge hill was Humpback, which Montana Central was going to have to tunnel, provided they could get right-of-way across Hatter's acreage.

Rowdy sighed. All his luck hadn't clabbered after all. He'd intended heading from end-of-steel to Hatter's place, but he'd been sidetracked on the way. And now he stood looking upon the goal so inadvertently kept from him.

There was no sign of the missing horse in the country below him. Rowdy cached the saddle and other gear among the rocks and made better time unburdened, coming down from the ridge and striking overland as fast as his boots would let him. Once upon the plain, he found it to be less flat than it had appeared from above, a rolling country with the ranch buildings often lost to his sight, but with the huge upthrust of Humpback Hill to serve him always as a landmark. Noon came, and he crossed a creek and slaked his thirst and sat and rested himself, then took to walking again. He saw cattle grazing, good blooded stock, but no riders put in an appearance. Rowdy could have used a lift, but he was still afoot when he reached the ranch.

It was a sprawling place, built mostly of logs, hauled, doubtless, from the wooded slopes of the Weetigos; and there was a ranch-house, a barn, corrals, a bunk-house, and a few other buildings. The ranch-house was long and low, with a gallery running around three sides of it, and it was from the chimney of this building that the smoke rose. The crew was somewhere out upon the range, for only a few saddlers switched their tails listlessly in the corrals; and Rowdy, approaching the place obliquely and coming into the openness between the ranch-house and the other buildings, saw no signs of activity around the bunk-house.

Yet people were about; he could hear their voices coming from the front of the ranch-house.

Whereupon Rowdy paused to wonder how he should present himself. He knew little of Mad Hatter, except that the man was eccentric and stubborn and doubtless laid claim to his queer soubriquet. He also knew that the man was mightily opposed to the coming of the railroad; and Rowdy had to remember that he was a representative of that railroad, even though he was discredited in certain circles. But Western hospitality was a sturdy thing, and he was a bedraggled wayfarer with a claim upon that hospitality. He had walked many miles to get here, and he would have bargained away his soul for a plate of ham and eggs at this precise moment, so he boldly climbed to a wing of the gallery and stalked along—until he was arrested by a voice that was all too familiar.

Taisy was out there to the front of the gallery. And Taisy was saying vehemently, "If ever I lay eyes on him, I'll kill him!"

Me? Rowdy wondered.

"I can't blame you for your bitterness, child," a man's voice said. "But after all, that is long over and done with."

That was Abner Grubb talking! At first Rowdy was greatly astonished; he had not been surprised to find Taisy Hatter on the ranch which was her home, but he'd supposed that Grubb was in Tailholt. Still, the banker had had ample time to come here in the twenty-four hours since Rowdy had last seen him; yet the surprise was still there. Taisy said, "Over and done with? When the ranchers make a dummy of him once a year and hang it from the highest tree!"

"Wrath is slow to die," Grubb observed. "After all, Big Tom McMasters crippled this range badly. It has taken ten of the thirteen years for the cattlemen to recover from the blow Big Tom struck when he walked off with the funds of the bank. Now we're a prosperous people again. Soon the whole business will be forgotten."

"Not by me," said Taisy. "He robbed the ranchers, yes. But I'm the one he left fatherless and homeless and with a name that smells like skunk weed on this range. I tell you, if I ever lay eyes on him, I'll kill him!"

Rowdy stood stock-still. He knew now whom they were talking about; and he was remembering the other night when he and Stumpy had dashed to the rescue of a man being lynched, only to learn that it was an effigy that was doing an air-dance—an effigy of an absconding banker named Big Tom McMasters. Now he was learning more about this same Tom McMasters; and, a consuming curiosity upon him, he edged forward to the turn of the gallery and peeped around it.

Abner Grubb said, "Do you remember your father at all, Taisy?"

The thin, black-clad banker had come here by saddle horse; at least he had obviously used that mode of transportation from end-of-steel, for he was seated upon the lower steps of the gallery, holding the reins of a saddler lax in his hand. Taisy was perched above him, straddling the railing of the gallery. Rowdy could see only her profile, but it was stormy.

"I was five, going on six, when he lit out," Taisy said. "I remember a big, red-faced man with a booming laugh. Mostly, I remember that last night: he came in and kissed me. He mustn't 'a' shaved since morning, and his stubble tickled fierce. Then I remember people trooping through the house and me being taken to one place and another in town, and then Hatter coming and fetching me to this ranch."

Grubb sighed. "Poor Hatter. He made a good home for you and did the best he could, and he's to be commended. He was hit as hard as anyone by what happened to the bank. I know; I was the cashier at the time."

"He gave me a name," Taisy said staunchly. "A name I didn't have to be ashamed of. I'm hoping some day people will forget I'm really a McMasters."

"They'd forget it sooner if you were Mrs. Abner Grubb."

"You courtin' me again? I thought you come here on business for that pesky railroad."

Grubb coloured slightly. "It's true that I want to discuss right-of-way with Hatter when he's finished his nap. And I did promise Mark Champion I'd try again to persuade Hatter to let the rails cross his land. But I wanted to visit you as well, Taisy. Why do you suppose I've been fetching the mail as an excuse to stop out this way whenever I could? By the way, you're rather interested in young Champion, aren't you?"

"He's got a nice smile," Taisy said reflectively.

"But a job that keeps him constantly on the fringes of the frontier. Wouldn't you rather a home in Tailholt, Taisy? My house is big, you know."

"You're old enough to be my father," Taisy said bluntly.

"The more reason I'd make you a good husband," Grubb said without rancour. "You see, Taisy, I've known you since your childhood. I know that you're wild and unpredictable, and perhaps more than a touch of Tom Mc-Masters is in you. But we'd live that down together, you and I."

Taisy withdrew a leg from over the gallery railing and came to stand upon the porch, her voice furious. "I don't want your blasted pity! I don't need it! I'm a Hatter, do you understand? And a Hatter is as good as anybody!"

"Now, Taisy——!" Grubb remonstrated.

Give him hell, gal! Rowdy thought gleefully.

Taisy said in a quieter voice, "You've been a mighty good friend, Abner. I just got to think some more about getting married."

Grubb said, a trace of anger in his tone, "You were less indecisive before Champion came here to put the spur through."

Taisy said dreamily, "His hair kinda curls."

Grubb frowned, and a heavy silence fell, and out of it Grubb finally said, "Taisy, I've never told this to you—or to anyone else—but I happen to know your father's whereabouts."

Taisy was instantly stiff with anger. *"You know!"*

"It has troubled my conscience for several years. You see, Tom McMasters was both my friend and my employer. He made me cashier of the bank, and he treated me kindly. When he absconded, my own small savings were part of the money he took; yet my bitterness was tempered by the remembrance of the things he'd done for me. One reason why I pitched in and worked so hard when the bank became mine, after he left, was that I wanted to make the bank something for this range to be proud of; so people who'd lost their money might feel less bitter against Tom. And now the bank is sound again."

"But you said you know where the damn' skunk is," Taisy persisted.

Grubb nodded. "A few years ago I got a letter from him. From one of the Central American countries—never mind which one. He said he was healthy and reasonably happy; I got the impression he'd been greatly troubled by remorse. He asked about you, but I never answered the letter. For many nights I paced the floor wrestling with my conscience, over whether I should hand that letter to the law. Yet, in spite of everything, that would have been like betraying a friend. Finally I checked into the law; he couldn't be extradited from the country to which he'd fled. So I said nothing to anyone—until to-day."

Taisy said very slowly, "Some day I'll make you tell me where he is. And then I'll go down there and find him."

"Some day," said Grubb, "you'll forget all this. I don't know why you keep brooding about it."

Taisy said, "I think I hear Dad Hatter stirring. You want to palaver with him, don't you?"

Grubb said, "I'd better."

It was high time, Rowdy decided, that he put in an appearance, and so he chose to be done with his eavesdropping. He had learned this one astonishing thing: Taisy Hatter was in reality Taisy McMasters and mighty bitter about it, but of what use that knowledge could ever be, Rowdy didn't know. He would have much preferred to have had the conversation turn to that mysterious spur which had gone eastward from this ranch, but obviously the talk between Taisy and the banker had terminated.

And so Rowdy coughed and stepped boldly around the corner—and thus ran into the unexpected.

His brief encounters with Taisy Hatter had been none too happy affairs, and he hardly supposed she would greet him with open arms on this occasion. But it was Grubb whose reactions were surprising. Grubb had his look at Rowdy and instantly reared himself to a stand, surprise and anger on his bony face. "Dow!" he snapped. "So you're here! You damn' turncoat renegade!"

Now Rowdy had had no liking for Abner Grubb from the first, but he hadn't figured the banker to be a man of action or a man of violence, and he was caught flat-footed by the suddenness of Grubb's move, for the banker's hand vanished beneath his rusty black coat and appeared with a Colt forty-five in it, the man thumbing back the hammer in the same motion. Grubb was going to shoot, and there was nothing for Rowdy to do but reach for his own hardware; but Grubb had the edge on him. Grubb was tilting the barrel, and Rowdy might have fumbled for an appropriate prayer, but at that precise moment a voice spoke from the doorway of the ranch-house.

"Stop it, Grubb!" the voice ordered. "If there's a killing to be done on this ranch, I'll do it!"

And that, Rowdy sensed, was Mad Hatter speaking.

Considering what he'd heard of the legend of Mad Hatter, Rowdy might have expected a two-headed man, ten feet tall, with his teeth filed to sharp points. Certainly he'd presumed that Hatter would be tousled of mane, wild-eyed, and doubtless prone to homicide on the slightest provocation. Thus Rowdy was astonished at the sight of the man who stepped from the doorway, for Mad Hatter looked like no maniac. Quite the contrary.

True, Hatter was huge, and his hair, silvery grey, was long and shaggy, but it was neatly brushed back from a high forehead, and about Hatter was a simple dignity that was at once unobtrusive and commanding. The man wore range garb and had the look of whang leather to him. He would never see sixty again. His voice was calm; his eye was steady. He repeated, "Stop it, Grubb!"

It was the banker who had turned madman. The gun wavered in Grubb's hand, but he still had his finger on the trigger, and he still had his eyes fixed balefully upon Rowdy. Rowdy took a step forward. Grubb said, "This man's got murder chalked up against him, Hatter! He took employment with the railroad, but he was really working against Montana Central. He was held prisoner yesterday, and his long-riding friends came to his rescue last night. They tossed a few bullets around while they were at it. I came as far as end-of-steel this morning. You should see the camp! There were graves to be dug."

Hatter frowned. "The railroad's troubles are no concern of mine. I haven't wanted those thunder wagons snorting across the range, stinking up the air, and scaring the fat off good cattle."

"But you don't want murder done, either," Grubb argued. "You're just being stubborn, Lucius. You hate a turncoat—any kind of turncoat—as much as I do. I tell you, this man deserves killing!"

He levelled the gun again, and Hatter said in a thunderous voice, "Are you judge, jury, and executioner all in one?"

"He's slippery, and I've got him where I want him," Grubb snarled. "Not a man on this range would blame me for putting a bullet in him if they could see that construction camp this morning!"

Whereupon Rowdy became simultaneously aware of two things: Mad Hatter wore no gun; therefore it was up to Rowdy to save himself from the wrath of Grubb. That Grubb might be legitimately entitled to his wrath didn't enter into Rowdy's calculations. Rowdy had only one hide and he wasn't anxious to have it perforated. Now he took another step nearer Grubb and kicked desperately at the banker's gun. He was aware that Mad Hatter stood riveted just outside the doorway and that Taisy was making some sort of move towards Grubb, but at that moment Rowdy's boot toe was connecting with Grubb's wrist. The gun spoke, but the bullet went through the wooden awning over the gallery, and the gun flew out of Grubb's fingers.

Rowdy was instantly upon the man, wrapping his arms around Grubb and bearing him backwards down the steps, the two of them landing in a writhing heap on the ground where they were at once imperilled by the hoofs of Grubb's horse, which began prancing. But Rowdy was heedless of new danger; he had looked into the barrel of a six-shooter aimed at his own brisket, and red wrath commanded him. He had an advantage of youth over Grubb; but the banker was surprisingly wiry, and Grubb, too, was crazy angry. But Rowdy, breaking free of the man, hauled Grubb to his feet.

Across the yard stood a horse trough, and Rowdy

dragged Grubb towards it. The banker struggled in his grip; and Rowdy slapped him twice, stinging, open-handed blows, then got him to the trough and plunged him into it. Once, twice, a third time, he forced Grubb's head and shoulders down into the green, slimy water, then hauled the man from the trough and stood him on his feet.

"Pile on that horse!" Rowdy ordered. "Pile on, and make yourself scarce!"

The dripping, bedraggled banker spat out enough water to drown a small dog, glared wildly at Rowdy, and stumbled towards his horse. He caught up the reins and rose to the saddle, and Rowdy darted up the gallery steps and snatched Grubb's fallen gun from the planking. Jacking the bullets out of it, Rowdy handed the gun to Grubb. "The next time you get a notion to use that," Rowdy snapped, "you'd better think again!"

"I'll kill you for this!" Grubb said with icy fury and wheeled his mount and headed out of the yard.

Watching him go, Rowdy felt his wrath ebb; and he turned to find Hatter regarding him with a scowl and Taisy staring with her lips slightly parted and her eyes big with excitement. Rowdy grinned. "I like this place," he announced. "It keeps a man from getting rusty."

Neither Hatter nor his adopted daughter matched his grin. Hatter said thoughtfully, "It was your play and I guess you were entitled to your fun. But you've made an enemy."

"I've worked up an appetite, too," Rowdy said pointedly.

Hatter's scowl became one of slight bewilderment; he was obviously finding it difficult to peg Rowdy as a friend or enemy, and Rowdy's vast aplomb left the man puzzled. But Hatter made a gesture with his hand and said, "If you're hungry, come in. Taisy, will you make this man some breakfast?"

Taisy said, "Shucks, I'd feed *anybody* that was hungry."

"That's an admirable attitude," said Rowdy.

She led him into the ranch-house and Rowdy found

himself in a room of rawhide-bottomed chairs and home-made rag rugs, a room with the simplicity and dignity of Hatter himself. Seated, Rowdy covertly studied his host, who had also come into the room; but Hatter seemed to have forgotten that he had a guest. The man had dropped into a chair and absently picked a stockman's journal from a centring table; he idly turned the pages, his eyes vacant. Once he combed his mane with his fingers; and as he brushed back the silvery grey hair, Rowdy glimpsed a long, white scar which had been concealed.

That scar interested Rowdy; it indicated that the man had at one time received a head wound, and a bad one at that. Stumpy had once heard that Hatter had been hit by a horseshoe, but that scar was from a bullet wound, Rowdy decided. Yet Hatter was certainly not insane, in spite of his soubriquet. Rather, Rowdy judged, he was a man given to moods and abstractions, but some of his moods might well be violent ones. Rowdy felt slightly ill at ease with Hatter; he felt as though he, Rowdy, were not really here as far as Hatter was concerned, yet that Hatter might suddenly become explosively aware of him. It was with relief that Rowdy heard Taisy call from the adjacent kitchen: "Come and get it, or I'll feed it to the hawgs."

In the kitchen, Rowdy found bacon and eggs and coffee awaiting him, and he fell upon the food with gusto. Taisy stood watching him smokily, saying nothing, and the feeling of discomfiture Rowdy had felt in the living-room still clung to him. At last he asked politely, "Did your aunt come out with you?"

"Miss Arabella's still in Tailholt," Taisy said. "She won't come out here till she can fetch that spur along. And she ain't my aunt. She's Dad Hatter's cousin, which would make her second cousin to me, if we were blood kin. But you heard enough on the gallery waggling them big ears of your'n, to know that I ain't no Hatter, not really."

Rowdy said, "I couldn't help hearing a part of the talk."

Taisy's eyes blazed. "You ever go calling me a McMasters and I'll kill you!"

"Look," Rowdy said, laying down his knife and fork, "I don't give a hoot who you are. I heard something I wasn't supposed to hear. I won't be forgetting that it's none of my business."

Taisy softened. "Maybe I got my dander up when I shouldn't have." She regarded Rowdy for a long moment. "You're kinda cute."

"Sure! Babies and old ladies and lost puppy dogs take a great shine to me," said Rowdy. "By the way, you started to jump at Grubb when he was going to gun me down. I'm beholden for that."

"I didn't want no killing on our doorstep," said Taisy. "We try to keep this place clean."

Rowdy grinned. "Well, Grubb got a bath."

Taisy frowned. "If I know Abner Grubb, you're gonna be sorry you did that."

Rowdy emptied his coffee cup. "I'd like to talk to Hatter," he said. "About the railroad. You think he could be persuaded to give Montana Central right of way?"

Taisy's eyes brightened again. "Then you ain't really turned against the railroad? I think if you double-crossed Mark Champion I'd run you down the road till your pockets was gatherin' gravel."

"Grubb made a mistake," Rowdy said. "It was an honest mistake, likely; there was a time last night when *I* was beginning to wonder whose side I really was on. No, I'm not a turncoat. Thank you for the breakfast, miss. And now I'll go talk business with your dad."

"It ain't gonna please him none," Taisy prophesied.

But when Rowdy came back into the living-room, Mad Hatter was gone. Striding to the gallery, Rowdy saw the ranch owner riding away to the north-west; and though he shouted after the man, Hatter paid him no heed. Taisy came out to the gallery and stood watching. "He's gone to join the crew; they're mending fence," she said. "Better let him be. He'll come back later."

Rowdy sighed. "Do you play checkers?"

"Me, I've got riding to do myself. You make yourself at home. We never threw anybody offen the place yet till they did something to get throwed. If you've got to see Dad, I don't suppose I can budge you."

"You sure make me feel right at home!" said Rowdy.

Thereafter, he occupied himself with the stockman's journals while Taisy left, to cross the yard later aboard a horse. This railroad work, Rowdy reflected dismally, consisted mostly of roundsiding, with intermittent flashes of action that stirred up a little excitement while they lasted but seemed to get him nowhere. His objective had been to reach Hatter and talk right of way with the man, and by a round-about trail he had reached Hatter's ranch. But the man had absented himself, and there was nothing for Rowdy to do but await his return. Surrendering philosophically, Rowdy put in an aimless afternoon.

Taisy returned towards sundown and made supper for herself and Rowdy which they ate in silence. Lamps were lighted; and Taisy, obviously in a sombre mood, busied herself about the house. At last Rowdy said, "I think I'll head out to the bunk-house. Hatter keeps late hours."

Taisy said very solemnly, "I been thinking it over. You'd better light out of here. I'll give you the loan of a horse."

Rowdy said, "Now see here! Do you think that after waiting all day——?"

"I saw Abner Grubb while I was out riding," Taisy said. "He's still hanging around. I got a notion why. You made him a laughing stock when you dumped him in the horse trough. Abner ain't the kind to forgive something like that. I'll bet he's still simmering."

"I'm not afraid of Grubb," Rowdy retorted.

"It's Dad I'm really worried about," Taisy said. "He's got into one of his moods. I could see it before he left. It ain't you I'm concerned about, mister; it's what might happen to Dad if the two of you tangled."

"I can talk sense into him," Rowdy insisted.

"You don't know him," she said. "He has trouble with his head; it hurts him mighty fierce sometimes. And he can't remember things, and he tries awful hard. He don't know how to peg you, but either you're a railroader or a long-rider and he ain't got much liking for either. I wouldn't want him to come home a-pawin' sod and get mixed up with you."

"You mean I've wore out my welcome?"

"Mister," said Taisy, "I ain't too sure about you myself. But if you're working for Mark Champion and anything happened to you, I don't reckon Mark would like that. I'm trying to help you, you mule-headed fool. I got a hunch there could be trouble for you here tonight, either from Dad or from Abner Grubb. You'd best get on your way."

"Look," said Rowdy, "I didn't land here wrapped in a wreath of roses. I've *had* trouble, miss. I'm not leaving till I try doing business with Hatter."

Taisy sighed. "Looks like I'll have to get my bull whip and run you off the place."

"Well," said Rowdy, "if you put it that way——By the way, where does Hatter sleep?"

Taisy was startled into an instinctive answer. "In there," she said, jerking her shoulder towards an adjacent room. Then: "What do you care where he sleeps?"

"Just curious," said Rowdy. "Where's that horse you're loaning me?"

"Where do you suppose?" said Taisy and led him out upon the gallery and around the house to the corrals. Here she plied a ketch rope and got gear on to a horse for him, and when she handed him the reins, she said, "You can come back some other time. You tell Mark I took good care of you."

Rowdy said, "Thanks for everything," and neck-reined out of the yard.

He rode away, holding the horse to a steady walk and not once looking back, hoping to lend the impression of a man surrendering to the inevitable, yet he had no intention of quitting the Hatter ranch. Not really. Taisy had been determined to send him on his way, though whether her fears were based on no more than woman's intuition he couldn't tell. He'd seen the futility of arguing with her, so he'd made this pretence of acquiescence. But he had business with Hatter—and with Hatter he was determined to talk. A man had to do something to earn his pay.

Heading almost due east, he crossed the rolling terrain over which he had stumbled afoot this morning, making much better time now, and it was not long before he found himself in the shadow of the rimrock ridge that marked the beginning of the canyon country—the ridge from which he'd spied Hatter's place early that day. Here he reined short, holding the horse in a pocket of darkness and sitting his saddle. From this vantage point he could watch the ranch-house and, specifically, the darkened window of the room which Taisy had indicated was Mad Hatter's. Sooner or later lamplight would spring from that window, and by that token Rowdy would know that Hatter had returned.

And so he waited, an hour running its slow course. The night was moonless and only a few stars showed. He was toying with the notion of shaping up a cigarette when he heard a horse nicker nearby. Instantly he was leaning forward and clamping his hand over the nostrils of his own mount to keep it from replying in kind. He had no idea what horseman moved in the night, but it might be Grubb. And then he heard the rattle of loose gravel and the creak of saddle leather; and he knew that not one but many men were here, pocketing him.

By intent, or accident? He couldn't be sure, nor could he do more than guess at the identity of these nocturnal riders. He wondered fleetingly if they were Hatter's crew, but Mad Hatter, when he'd ridden to join his crew, had headed in the opposite direction, towards the northwest. Railroad construction workers, still searching for him? But Rowdy doubted that such a search party would be mounted. And so by the process of elimination he arrived at the truth. These men who moved in the darkness, surrounding him, were the raiders who had struck at the construction camp. He had lost them and found them again, and they were so close that the horse of one nudged against Rowdy's horse, and a man cursed softly, and Rowdy knew that he had been discovered.

Here was a time when either to fight or to run would be folly; Rowdy was both outnumbered and surrounded, so he merely sat his saddle and awaited the inevitable. He had a gun—the gun he'd taken from the unhorsed marauder at the construction camp last night—but to reach for it would invite becoming as perforated as a Swiss cheese. A fine fix this was! Rowdy peered hard in the darkness, trying to count heads and estimate the odds. Then the man who had bumped into him said, "Move on, feller. We'd better string out or we'll be tramping each other."

That was when the thunderous truth struck Rowdy. He hadn't been recognised; this man who was almost on top of him presumed that Rowdy belonged to the group that had converged here. Rowdy touched heel to horse. Pocketed by the other riders, he moved out from beneath the overhang of the rimrock ridge as they went jogging down towards the flats upon which Hatter's ranch sprawled. He was like a piece of driftwood sucked up by the current. These men, riding down out of the canyon country in the deep darkness, had collected him without realising that he wasn't one of them.

How long this enforced ruse could be successfully maintained Rowdy didn't know, but it behooved him to play out the string. Any move to extricate himself would immediately arouse suspicion and bring disaster upon him, for he was now certain that he was in the midst of the railroad raiders. Here on the flat it was still too dark to distinguish a man's features, but Rowdy had made out the silhouette of the rider who took the lead and recognised the slope of that one's shoulders. He was the same big man who had thrust a gun under the nose of Miss Arabella Hatter when the stagecoach had been stopped, and Rowdy had seen him a second time when the construction camp was raided last night. No mistake about that.

Now the group—there were nearly a score of them—was strung out in an irregular double column; and Rowdy, by one ruse and another, kept dropping back until he was well to the rear. His hope was to fall behind and then take off at a tangent into the night, thus freeing himself of a companionship as welcome as a hornets' nest in a Sunday hat. But opportunity was slow in coming to him. At last he swung down from his saddle, flung back his left stirrup and made a pretence of tightening the cinch. He hoped that the others would ride on, leaving him under the presumption that he would hasten to overtake them; but the group came to a stop.

"Hurry it up, feller!" the nearest man ordered impatiently.

Rowdy was instantly sorry he'd thus focused attention upon himself. This made a bad moment. His garb, pearl-buttoned shirt and foxed trousers, was a little more pretentious than most; and some of these men might have night eyes. He hoped there were a few dandies in the group so that he wouldn't be too conspicuous. His breath was tight in his throat as he mounted again. He felt like a man fussing with the heels of a mule.

But at least the night was his ally, and he began to reason that many of these men might well be strangers to each other. That such a large force had appeared in the Weetigos to harass Montana Central argued that they'd been fetched from afar, probably from many different points. But shortly the moon was apt to be showing itself, and to-night that jolly beacon of the sky would be just as welcome to Rowdy as a cattle rustler at a stockman's banquet. Yet there was nothing to do but ride along. His position was somewhat comparable to that of the unfortunate gentleman who'd got a catamount by the tail. Couldn't hang on—couldn't let go.

Soon they were nearing Hatter's ranch. Rowdy, involved in keeping himself unrecognised, had forgotten the vigil he'd been maintaining beneath the rimrock; but he took a look at the place now and saw that light had appeared in Hatter's bedroom. The ranch crew had got back, but Rowdy was not going to be able to spring a surprise visit upon Mad Hatter to-night.

Whereupon he resigned himself to the recent turn of events and decided to make the most of it. Last night he'd thought to trail these men and had been circumvented by the storm and the appearance of the dinosaur, but now the raiders had practically adopted him. Just went to show that a man made the most haste by standing still! But at least he was working for the railroad again; these men were the enemies of Montana Central, and it behooved Rowdy to discover what they were about. Doubtless it would be nothing to gladden the heart of a Sunday School teacher, but a man might learn something if he kept his eyes and ears open.

Rowdy was doing both. But abruptly the group drew to a halt as the man in the lead reined up. Slouching in his saddle, the broad-shouldered leader said, "I been thinking. Was we to scatter a few bullets at Hatter's place, he might figger it was railroaders giving him trouble. It wouldn't make him any happier about Montana Central."

"Hell, Pocatello," somebody said. "Why go buying us a fight when we got other orders?"

"Just a notion," said Pocatello. "Maybe you're right."

"That Hatter outfit is plumb salty," observed the other.

The group rode on, giving Hatter's place a wide berth. Rowdy kept his sombrero tugged low and his chin against his chest; and whenever a stirrup partner spoke to him, he answered with a grunt. He'd given up trying to elude these men. He hoped to find out who their paymaster was. Pocatello was the leader, but Pocatello took his orders from someone else. That had been indicated by the brief conversation anent Hatter's place. Rowdy could have made a guess concerning Pocatello's boss, remembering the wisp of white silk that had clung to the side of a stagecoach. But was Doctor Quong truly the king wolf or merely another hireling of someone higher up?

Such musings could lead only to a headache, so Rowdy gave them up.

Having circled Hatter's place, the riders bore due west, the bulk of Humpback Hill looming before them and growing bigger as they drew nearer. The belated moon finally showed itself, rising up out of the canyon country and taking a cautious peek at the landscape; but before it was high enough to throw any appreciable light, the riders were into the timber which covered the slopes of Humpback.

Here they went single-filing along a twisting trail, and Rowdy might have easily fallen behind if he had been the last man. But by now he was tingling with the prospect of playing this hand out. Perhaps he was a fool who was inviting his own early demise from this vale of vicissitudes, but the spirit of adventure had thoroughly possessed him. He thought of Stumpy who had cautioned him to take care of himself. Perhaps this escapade was one of those 'dobe dollars Stumpy had warned him to be leery of.

They began climbing, and sometimes they were forced to dismount and lead their horses; the timber grew thicker around them, pressing against the trail like two sooty hands. A fine place this would be to meet a dinosaur, Rowdy reflected. Then they were bursting into a clearing; and here, upon a rocky shelf on the east slope of Humpback, a tent stood against the bare face of a cutbank. A fire burned before the tent, and a saddle and other gear were piled upon a blanket, but there was no sign of a human. Pocatello halooed softly and the shadows surrendered a small, dapper figure, the elusive Doctor Quong stepping into the rim of the firelight. Obviously, he had concealed himself at the sound of oncoming horsemen.

"Good-evening, gentlemen," said Doctor Quong, his smile bland and eternal.

Pocatello swung down from his saddle. "We got news for you, boss. Somebody hit the construction camp last night. A bunch of rannyhans about our size. They stirred up quite a ruckus while it lasted. The Chinks come a-swarming, but they run into one of them big critters with the horny backs. There was considerable of a stampede."

Quong's smile grew to encompass all of the night. "Is good," he decided.

The men were spilling into the rim of the firelight, and Rowdy found himself dreading that puny blaze as intensely as Stumpy dreaded the dry state of Kansas. Not only might he be recognised now, but the Hatter cayuse he rode might be recognised as well—which would be just as disastrous. Men were dismounting and pulling gear from their horses, and Rowdy reluctantly did likewise, taking a great deal of time at the task. The horses were hazed beyond the firelight into a large rope corral. Rowdy slapped his mount inside and let his gear lie. This done he kept back in the shadows, moving aimlessly away whenever anyone came near him.

Pocatello, striding up to the fire, said, "What's next, boss?"

"I have an assignment which requires a prodigious amount of back-bending," Quong said, "so I have summoned all of you. Fortunately I am equipped with the proper tools. A palaeontologist is expected to be a purchaser of picks and shovels. You are about to become miners, my gentle friends. Each and every one of you."

Pocatello scowled. "What the blazes are you talking about? We hired on as fighting men!"

"And you shall receive the pay of fighting men," Quong said soothingly. "Is not that the important point?

And speaking of pay, you are all entitled to a reward for last night's work. I have money here. If you will kindly form a line and pass before me——"

He bobbed inside the tent and came forth with a canvas sack which seemed heavy in his hand and which jingled most promisingly. The men, showing a notable eagerness, began quickly to form into a line; and again Rowdy felt that tightening of his breath in his throat. To make any effort to avoid placing himself in the pay-line would be a most damning act; to join in the line and march into the rim of the firelight and present himself before Doctor Quong would be equally disastrous. Quong's memory wasn't so short that he'd have forgotten his fellow passenger of the day before yesterday.

Whereupon Rowdy found himself in the tightest of split sticks; but at that precise moment a voice called from the darkness beyond, halooing the camp; and every man stiffened, turning upon his heel and dropping his hand to his gun-butt. Only Doctor Quong remained as serene as ever.

"Quong!" the voice called from the brush. "This is Abner Grubb. I've got a gun in my hand and I've got it lined on your belly. Can I come in under a flag of truce and walk out the same way?"

Quong made a flourishing bow. "You are welcome as the gentle rain which blesses the thirsty hills," he said.

The bushes stirred faintly, and the black-garbed, stoop-shouldered banker appeared, walking towards the firelight with his hands before him, his hands empty. Pocatello and his men stood watching him, scowling blackly; but to these lesser lights Abner Grubb paid no heed. He faced Quong, and a mighty anger was in Abner Grubb, shaking his voice. "We'll dispense with preludes, Quong. You've got the spur?"

Again Quong bowed. "I have the spur," he conceded.

"Then we won't beat around the bush. How much do you want for it?"

Quong had placed the canvas money sack upon the ground; he reached within his coat, and his yellow hand came forth with an object wrapped in a white silk handkerchief—possibly that same handkerchief he had cherished so carefully aboard the stagecoach. He removed the handkerchief in the manner of a magician, and the firelight glinted upon the spur, and Rowdy leaned forward eagerly. From where he stood the spur appeared to be an ordinary one, no different from a thousand others. But Abner Grubb was staring at it like a man hypnotised, breathing hard and choked for words.

Then Grubb said again, "How much?"

Quong's shrug was no more than a shadow of a gesture. "I am at a disadvantage. Perhaps you have a greater knowledge of the value of this object than I. Shall we say fifty thousand dollars?"

Grubb almost strangled. "That's crazy!"

"Is it?" Quong said softly. "Very well. Perhaps I can find another prospective purchaser who is less penurious."

The same mad wrath that had consumed Grubb on Hatter's gallery earlier in the day consumed him now, and he took a lunging step forward. "Give me that, you dirty, yellow, double-dealing skunk!" he stormed. "Give it to me, I say!"

Quong stepped back a pace, quailing not at all; and though his voice was as bland as ever, Rowdy had the feeling that the devil was laughing inside the Chinaman. "Easy, my impetuous friend," said Quong. "Need I remind you that your affiliation with Montana Central is well known? Or that these men who surround you are hired to strike at Montana Central in any way that will do the railroad harm?" He was convulsed with silent laughter. "You appreciate the shakiness of your position, Mr. Grubb, I'm sure."

"I appreciate the fact that you've got me exactly where you want me," Grubb said in a calmer voice. "But I'm not packing any fifty thousand dollars."

"Is it not true," Quong persisted, "that you wish the spur because with it you might persuade Mad Hatter to allow Montana Central right of way across his ranch? Surely, Mr. Grubb, the price is not too exorbitant, considering the prize."

In Rowdy was a conviction that Quong was playing a cat-and-mouse game with Abner Grubb, the exact nature of which was known only to the two men. In each thing Quong had said there'd seemed to lurk a double meaning. But torturing Rowdy now was a great desire and a great temptation. He had caught up with that will-o'-the-wisp, the phantom spur; it was almost within reach of his hand.

Suppose he should dash forward and wrest it from Quong's grasp? That would be easy enough. The problem would be to get away from this camp afterwards. Yet the temptation was overpowering, and he was edging forward when he found a man at his elbow. This man was peering hard, for Rowdy had now ventured within the firelight's rim. Suddenly the man batted at Rowdy's sombrero, knocking it from his head.

"Say, who the hell are you?" the man demanded, and thus Rowdy stood revealed as an intruder. He swung his fist at the fellow and missed, and the man closed with him. A dozen men came converging from everywhere, and pandemonium ruled the camp.

11 : A Hero is Born

On his second morning in Tailholt, Stumpy Grampis sat in Montana Central's office in the Odd Fellows building, a man satisfied with the world. A transformation had come over Stumpy. A floppy sombrero now rested upon his ears, and he wore a dirt-glazed shirt, and a pair of Levis so stiff with long absence from a tub that they could have stood in a corner and defended themselves against all comers. Completing the ensemble was a pair of boots, run over at the heels, and spurs with rowels the size of wagon wheels. Stumpy was garbed to his liking; and he sat with his chair tilted precariously and his spurs hooked on the edge of the conference table, paring the while at his fingernails with a jacknife as big as a cavalry sabre. Stumpy was at peace.

Not so Mark Champion. The railroad's chief construction engineer paced nervously from table to window, pausing often to gaze down into the street; and Bartholomew B. Bartholomew shared Champion's agitation. Little Launcelot, also present, had his nose buried in a book and was lost to the world, a factor which contributed to Stumpy's wellbeing. Between these two stood an armed truce, but Stumpy had become wary. Launcelot, in Stumpy's estimation, was to be considered with the same caution one bestowed upon a sleeping sidewinder.

Launcelot set the book aside with a yawn. "Chaucer," he observed, "had a most obvious humour. Almost infantile. Personally, I prefer Rabelais. And you, Mr. Grampis?"

"You itchin' for an argument?" Stumpy demanded.

Mark Champion paused in his striding. "We've got

enough troubles," he announced. "Come to the window
and have a look. More coolies pouring in from end-of-
steel! I tell you, they're deserting in droves! And all I can
get out of those I've talked to is *dragon—dragon*! How am I
going to build a spur if I haven't got labourers?"

B. B., his florid face creased with worry, said, "Why in
blazes doesn't McAllister send in a coherent report? Or
Dow? Something happened out there last night; we know
that. Can't they understand that we might like full de-
tails?"

"Now don't you go frettin' about Rowdy," Stumpy put
in. "He's likely got the situation well in hand."

"Grubb went out to end-of-steel early this morning,"
Champion observed. "Maybe he'll be back to-day to tell us
what's going on. McAllister must have his hands full. All
he wired was 'CAMP RAIDED DURING STORM
BEASTIE WALKING AGAIN.' "

Bartholomew said, "Chicago won't be so sparse with
words. When we report this, they'll probably call off construction. It will take weeks to gather more coolies. Champion, this delay is going to be a black mark against my
record!"

"Easy, *pater,*" Launcelot advised. "After all, you have
that handsome watch they gave you for thirty years of
faithful service. I doubt if they'll take *that* back when they
send you down the road."

"Quiet!" B. B. bellowed. "I ought to be on my way to
San Francisco; that's what I ought to be doing. To recruit
more Chinese."

"Wa-al, now," Stumpy said reflectively, an idea stirring within him, "if more Chinks will solve your problem,
me, I've got a whizzer of a notion."

"Ha! Ha! Ha!" said Launcelot.

"Man," said B. B. with the look of one lost, "if you've
got any kind of notion, for land sakes let's hear it!"

But now there was a flurry of excitement in the anteroom beyond, the voice of the clerk rising quaveringly; and

time might have turned backward twenty-four hours; for Miss Arabella Hatter came bursting into the conference room, her hat askew and her blue eyes flashing angrily behind her square, steel-rimmed spectacles. The only difference was that she was unaccompanied to-day. Taisy Hatter was not along, but Miss Arabella nursed an anger large enough for the two of them.

"Look at you!" she stormed. "Standing there so serene as though there wasn't a bit of trouble in the world!"

"I assure you, ma'am," protested B. B., "that——"

"None of your glib talk!" the spinster interjected. "Do you think I'm blind to the deplorable conditions which infest this town. And to think that the railroad sanctions them! As a stockholder——"

"If you're here about that spur again——" B. B. began.

"The spur? That's important, too, but I'm concerned with the depravity that is rampant in Tailholt. Do you realise that every other building dispenses intoxicating beverages? And more saloons are springing up to take care of the railroad trade! I insist, sir, that you take steps at once to close all such institutions! Don't argue! If you forbid liquor to your workers, these emporiums of evil will have to shut their doors."

Bartholomew groaned. "The Chinese stampeding because of dragons, and *she* wants liquor forbidden to the Irish! We'll have no workers at all!"

"Better that than contributing to their debauchery," Miss Hatter insisted. "To think that my money has been invested with a corporation which deliberately allows wickedness to flourish! I tell you, Chicago shall have a long letter from me. Shall it say, Mr. Bartholomew, that you insist on championing licentiousness?"

B. B. placed his hands to his forehead and rocked upon his feet. "Don't write!" he cried. "I've got troubles enough. I'll see what I can do about—er—closing the saloons."

"That's better," said Miss Hatter, somewhat mollified. "I have your promise?"

"You have my promise."

"There goes the *pater*," Launcelot reflected, "leading with his chin again."

Miss Hatter backed toward the door. "I'll be waiting for results. Good day, gentlemen."

"That there woman has got plumb onsocial notions," Stumpy observed with a scowl.

"Never mind about her," B. B. said hastily. "I'd have promised her the moon to get her out of here! The thing I want to know is what sort of inspiration you had about replenishing our crews."

"Hop Gow," said Stumpy.

"Eh?" said B. B.

"Hop Gow lives in Helena. Friend o' mine. Has a sideline of smuggling other Chinks across the border. Immigration quotas being restricted in this country but, not in Canady, Hop Gow does a right pert business. Montana folks like Chinks for house servants."

A great hope blossomed in B. B.'s eyes. "You mean this Hop Gow might be able to supply us with workmen? At once?"

"Likely," said Stumpy. "He's got aliens hid under every rock between here and the border."

Launcelot yawned. "Stripes wouldn't suit you, *pater*. With your figure, you'd look as broad as all out doors."

"Chicago will square this with the government," B. B. mused. "They can get the aliens temporary permits to allow them in this country until the spur is finished. I'll see that your Chinese friend's name is kept out of it, Grampis."

"Hop Gow would figger it a nice stroke of business."

Bartholomew B. Bartholomew had become a man from whom a tremendous weight had been lifted. He was galvanised to action. "I'll start things stirring," he boomed. "Champion, get the despatcher here at once. And we'll want a special train for Grampis. Just a locomotive will do. Grampis, you'll be leaving within the hour. I'll have the despatcher clear the track." He strode to a wall map and had a look. "You should make Helena by nightfall. I'll be depending on you, man. Do you realise that the fate of the spur rests upon your shoulders? I tell you, Montana Central will never forget the man who solves this problem for them!"

Stumpy began to swell visibly. "I'm your huckleberry," he said, snapping his jack-knife shut.

Even Champion had caught the enthusiasm of his superior. "I'll get the despatcher," he said, "and line up a locomotive. Then I'm heading to end-of-steel. I want to know what's going on out there."

"You be sure that track's clear," Stumpy said imperiously. "That there iron steed o' mine's just gonna *sweep* everything out of its way."

Launcelot yawned again. "You're sending a man to do a child's work," he said.

But for once Stumpy was impervious to a jibe, for this was Stumpy's great moment, and the glory of it had stuffed cotton in his ears. Moreover, Stumpy felt as magnanimous as a drunk with his pockets full of pay. He could forgive even Launcelot. He could forgive Rowdy for leaving him to round-side aimlessly while Rowdy had headed out to the fun. A crisis had risen, but Stumpy had towered above it. A name would shine in golden letters in the annals of Montana Central after this day. S-T-U-M-P-Y G-R-A-M-P-I-S. . . . Destiny had sneered in the past and treated Stumpy like a poor country cousin, but doubtless destiny had been preserving him for just such an emergency as this. The fate of the railroad rested in his horny hands.

"I'll git there and back," Stumpy said stoutly.

And so it came about that a despatcher's key clicked frantically and a locomotive was detached from a string of cars, and to its cab Stumpy mounted within the hour, empowered by Bartholomew B. Bartholomew to deal with

Hop Gow in the name of Montana Central. There wasn't a Stetson west of the river that would have fitted Stumpy. He gave a wave of his hand to Bartholomew and Champion and little Launcelot, who had seen him to the track; he gestured a peremptory order to engineer and fireman, who responded with scant enthusiasm. But steam hissed and the wheels began to turn, and Stumpy was off on his great mission.

"Bend over that shovel," Stumpy ordered the fireman. "Time's a-burnin'."

"Since when," demanded the fireman, "have railroads been run by fellers that stink of horses?"

Stumpy forgave the man. Doubtless Paul Revere had encountered sceptics on his historic ride. And the boy who'd stood on the burning deck had probably appeared to be just another mortal. But one day, when this fireman was old, the fellow would gather his grandchildren around his knees and tell them of Stumpy Grampis. "Knew him well," the fireman would say. "A great man, children; ordinary as an old shoe. . . ."

The locomotive picked up speed, and the countryside began to blur past. This was terrain such as Stumpy had traversed in the stagecoach the day before yesterday, and Stumpy was impatient to be beyond it and pitting himself against the mountain barrier between here and Helena.

The engineer was on his seat, his head craned from the window, his hand on the whistle cord. The fireman was bent to his task. Stumpy had been provided with a stool—with padding—and here he sat enthroned, his leathery face wearing the look of Jove.

"Can't you squeeze more speed outa this rattler?" he demanded.

An hour out of Tailholt they came upon a settlement where a freight train waited upon a siding. The despatcher had done his duty by destiny. Stumpy gave the freight's impatient engineer a generous wave. They rolled onward, the locomotive belching smoke which bannered against the sky, steam screaming from the pistons as the drivers pounded over the unlevelled rails. They streaked across the miles to the main line, and after that they began climbing, and then it seemed to Stumpy that they slowed to a pace that would have had a tortoise pawing the sod. He belaboured the fireman, drawing copiously upon his amazing vocabulary.

"Look," said the sweating recipient of this blistering barrage, "there's a spare shovel in the cab. If you want more speed, start heaving coal."

"Some," said Stumpy loftily, "are born into this world to work with their backs. Some with their brains."

"What's that got to do with you and me?" asked the fireman.

They made it to the top of the divide as dusk settled; they came roaring down the far slant with the headlamp pencilling the night, but at the bottom of the slope the engineer applied the brakes so suddenly that Stumpy's sombrero tipped down over his eyes. They slid to a screeching stop at a small depot. Stumpy was at once fit to be tied. The local despatcher appeared out of the night and silently handed the engineer train orders. That worthy spoke to the fireman, who got out to switch them on to a siding.

"That semaphore was red," the engineer told Stumpy. "Someone wired ahead and had us sidetracked."

"The track was supposed to be cleared!" Stumpy howled. "You want Montana Central ruint?"

"We're off our own line. This is Northern Pacific's track," the engineer explained. "Maybe Montana Central couldn't get them to clear for us. We're going to wait, and that's all there is to it."

"Here comes a train," the fireman announced.

A locomotive hurtled past them in the night; the semaphore blinked; they could move on. Far ahead they saw the red markers of the other train, and then these were gone. Stumpy was fairly dancing with frustration. "We gotta make up lost time!" he shouted. "We gotta get to Helena pronto!"

But Stumpy was battling the vast, complicated system of signals and communications by which the railroads are run, and the engineer was obdurate; and they were side-tracked again, this time to allow a special from the east to pass them, heading the opposite direction. Stumpy called upon the stars to witness this great stupidity, and thereafter he kept both engineer and fireman sweating. At last, in sheer desperation, Stumpy went to work with the spare shovel.

Thus they came chugging into Helena with the sweat rolling from Stumpy and coal grime streaking his face; but doubtless the boy who'd poked his fist into the dyke hadn't looked impeccable when his night's work was done. The engine wheezing into the yards, Stumpy was down from the cab and running before the wheels quit turning. He went panting along the tortuous streets of Montana's capital following the windings of Last Chance Gulch to the south, until he neared the faded shingle of Hop Gow, dealer in jade and tea.

Stumpy came to an abrupt stop, stricken with a horrible thought: Suppose Hop Gow weren't here? Suppose the rotund Celestial were up on the border, or perhaps gone to China? It had been many weeks since Stumpy had laid eyes on his friend. But Hop Gow *had* to be there! Destiny wouldn't choose a favourite child for greatness and then disown him!

Thus Stumpy stepped into the establishment expecting to find his moon-faced friend presiding behind the counter, but instead he was greeted by a bland Oriental who would have made only a thin shadow of his master.

Stumpy said breathlessly, "Where's Hop Gow?"

"Him there," said the nameless Chinese and indicated a curtained doorway.

Stumpy took a step in that direction.

"Him busy," said the man behind the counter. "Him entertaining distinguished glest."

"I got important business," Stumpy said. "For the railroad. We need a couple of hundred workers and——"

"All taken clare of," said the Chinese with a wave of his yellow hand.

"Taken care of——!" echoed the astounded Stumpy, and with a bound he was to the curtained doorway. Sweeping the curtain aside, he peered into a room resplendent with teakwood furnishings and many-hued lanterns, and saw seated upon a low divan Hop Gow and his distinguished guest. They made quite a study in contrast both in appearance and conduct. The corpulent Hop Gow had his opium pipe beside him and was roasting a pill on the end of a needle. His guest, angelic in Lord Fauntleroy suit, had a bowl of milk before him and was busily breaking crackers into it.

Looking up, little Launcelot said, with a great show of surprise. "Why, it's Mr. Grampis!"

"Stumpy Grampis!" cried Hop Gow, with a broad grin. "You looking older every day!"

But Stumpy was ignoring Hop Gow, for his eyes were fixed dazedly upon little Launcelot, and Stumpy was remembering that locomotive that had sped past them, headed this direction, the first time they'd been sidetracked. "You ordered us held up!" Stumpy bawled. "You tangled my twine after the despatcher cleared the track!"

Launcelot dipped spoon into cracker bowl. "Morse code is very simple," he said. "I learned it in my infancy. Whenever I wanted more mush, I used to beat upon my high-chair with my spoon—in dots and dashes. It was no trouble, Mr. Grampis, to countermand some of the despatcher's orders."

"But this was *my* job!" Stumpy shouted.

Launcelot looked injured. "Don't you suppose *I* have an interest in the welfare of the railroad? The *pater* was in such a stew about getting more labourers that I thought it would please him if the job were done efficiently. All the arrangements are finished; Mr. Hop has agreed that workmen will be on their way by morning. Don't look so perturbed, Mr. Grampis. You had a nice ride out of it, didn't you?"

"This velly smart boy," Hop Gow beamed. "Him gleat student of Confucius."

A mighty rage consuming him, Stumpy took a belligerent step forward, then stopped. Hop Gow, he judged, wouldn't stand for having his distinguished guest maimed before his eyes; and moreover Stumpy was blocked in another fashion. One couldn't spank a hero. And it was Launcelot Bartholomew, not Stumpy Grampis, who'd made himself a hero this day. Destiny—or was it little Launcelot?—had again fetched Stumpy a kick in the pants, and the difficulty was that Stumpy couldn't kick back.

12 : Pursued

To Rowdy, fighting valiantly against the converging men at Quong's camp, there came the feeling that he had bitten off considerably more than he could chew. But, exposed by the one who'd batted the sombrero from Rowdy's head, he had no choice but to try to get in a few licks before he was overpowered. Wrenching free of the man who had closed with him, Rowdy again swung his fist, and this time his knuckles connected with the fellow's stubbled jaw. The man went down, and two others who were rushing at Rowdy tripped over the fallen one, and thus for a second Rowdy had respite from his chores.

In that brief instant, the whole scene stood out with startling clarity—the tent against the bare face of the cutbank, the tiny fire, the figure of Quong who danced in excitement, still clutching the spur as he barked shrill orders, the heaped saddles and the milling men, and, on the far rim of the light, Abner Grubb standing petrified. Grubb had come here to pit himself against Quong, yet Rowdy looked for no help from the banker. Grubb was his enemy, too, and therefore one more to be weighed in the odds.

Then Rowdy became a busy little bee, for the men were coming at him again. He tried for his gun, but someone swarmed upon him, locking arms around Rowdy and Rowdy's thumb rasped futilely along his cartridge belt. Plucking a few shells from the belt, Rowdy hurled them into the heart of the fire. Then he was busy fending off the man who'd piled upon him; the two went down, rolling over and over again, in imminent peril of careening into the fire, but once more Rowdy broke free and got to a stand.

His advantage was that so many were pitted against him that they got in each other's way. Nor could they try gunning him down for fear of hitting each other. Quong, still hopping in excitement, was shouting: "Shoot! Shoot!" Gun barrels flashed in the firelight, but the sign wasn't right.

It might have been, for Rowdy stood alone for an instant, his chest heaving; then two men were upon him, struggling to bear him to the ground again. One was Pocatello, and him Rowdy favoured with a short punch to the midriff that brought the breath whooshing out of the man. The other was dragging at Rowdy, pulling him down by sheer weight; but suddenly the cartridges in the fire began popping. The general confusion was considerably increased by this little sideshow. Men began darting in every direction; and guns spoke then, raking the darkness beyond the firelight.

Just went to show you, Rowdy observed, how the power of suggestion worked. These railroad raiders were convinced that they were being attacked.

"I'm hit!" one cried and cursed savagely.

And to Rowdy's astonishment, he saw a man clutch at his arm, blood seeping between his fingers. The power of suggestion? Suddenly Rowdy realised that someone else was actually out there in the darkness, peppering this camp with bullets. Stumpy? Rowdy wasted little time on fruitless speculation. For a moment the balance had been swung; these railroad raiders were too occupied to be concentrating solely on him, and in that moment Rowdy leaped towards the fire and kicked at it frantically, scattering the embers and sending the smoke billowing.

Now he was just a faceless figure in a milling mass of panicked men, but he had marked an objective for himself, and scooping up his fallen sombrero and clapping it on his head he leaped towards his objective, his eyes smarting from the smoke, his throat feeling clogged. He got his hands on a diminutive form, and a shrill squeal told him it was the man he sought. Doctor Quong fought like a captured cat, but Rowdy kept his arms wrapped around the Chinese, and he felt along the man's arm to the wrist and twisted hard. Then Rowdy was down upon his hands and knees, groping, and his fingers closed over the spur.

He had the spur and he had freedom of a sort. The camp was still gripped in pandemonium, the scattered embers of the fire winking fitfully, the only light coming from gun flashes as the railroad raiders peppered aimlessly at the darkness. Still on his hands and knees, Rowdy scurried off; he kept going until he came to bushes, and he wormed into these and got to a stand. For a moment he stood listening, and then he headed away from the camp as fast as his legs could carry him.

He began moving along the timbered shoulder of Humpback Hill, seeking out a trail; and although he congratulated himself on his escape, he knew he was far from able to draw a truly free breath. He had in his possession the spur upon which Doctor Quong had set a price of fifty thousand dollars, and Quong would be in no mood to forget the whole matter. Shortly, as soon as Quong could organise his men, they'd be on the hunt for Rowdy, whose cue was to make himself as scarce as possible while time permitted. And so he kept moving, clawing through underbrush, striving to increase the distance between the camp and himself.

Again he paused to listen. Guns still popped, and he was gratified to observe that the sounds were much fainter. He hoped that a considerable force was holding Quong's camp under siege, but he realised this hope was futile. No more than one or two men had been shooting, the impression of a larger attacking force having been given by those cartridges popping in the fire. Abner Grubb? Had the banker faded back into the night and turned his gun against Quong's camp? Rowdy decided not. He still couldn't grab on to the notion of Grubb backing *him*. Still, Quong and his men were enemies of Grubb's, and perhaps the banker had seen in the situation a chance to make a play for the spur himself.

Speculation being as fruitless as a clothes-line pole, Rowdy gave it up and commenced moving again. He found a trail of sorts and followed it, gratified that it seemed to be looping downwards. He wanted to get off Humpback and head towards Hatter's place, but at least the hill was timbered and thus provided shelter. But now, when he paused to listen and to catch his breath, he was sure he heard horses moving through the brush. That would be Quong's crew, up into saddles and spreading out to search for him. Rowdy's hand tightened on the spur, and he thrust the object inside his shirt. He'd got the spur—blast the whole bunch of 'em!—and he'd give them a time getting it away from him!

But they were mounted and he was afoot, and therein the difference lay. Moreover, they might know this country far better than he did, though he guessed that the odds were about even on that score. The railroad raiders were imported men, which meant that this would be strange terrain to them too. Then as the realisation grew on him that his pursuers had fanned out, he sensed their strategy. They were flinging a wide loop of horsemen, hoping to encircle him, and in due course they'd only have to draw that loop tight to ensnare him. He judged that riders were above and below him; he heard them calling to one another; and he sensed how inevitable it was that sooner or later they would stumble upon him.

He could worm into the brush, of course, and just lie low. But daylight would eventually come, and hunger and thirst would drive him from cover. No it was better to plunge onward, to try to break through the circle and work downhill and make his way to Hatter's. So thinking, he moved steadfastly, tripping over deadfall logs, keeping away from the trail now, since any trail might be teeming with horsebackers.

He stayed in the brush until suddenly there was no brush, for a rockslide had at one time swept down the east slope of Humpback, starting somewhere above the point where Rowdy came upon the slide, and he had either to turn back or to clamber across the naked face of the slide and get to the brush on its far side. He made his choice quickly. No horse could pick its way over that littered stretch, so he went stumbling out upon the spilled rocks.

The moon had become obscured by clouds, but his eyes had grown accustomed to the darkness and there was starlight enough to make his progress easier than it might have been. Since he wanted to reach the bottom of the hill, he began groping down the face of the slide, at the same time moving laterally towards the brush on its far side.

Would Quong's crew be stopped by this rubble heap? Some of them might leave horses behind and make a search afoot. Rowdy paused often to listen, and sometimes he was sure other humans were close by. But they were pursuing their search in silence, and this silence became a clamour in Rowdy's ears. And then, moving around a huge boulder, he almost collided with a dim figure.

At once Rowdy's arms encircled the man; and for a moment they tussled silently, Rowdy bringing pressure on the man's ribs until the fellow cried out. It was that single ejaculation that gave Rowdy his cue. He knew that voice! He said, "Champion! That you, Mark?"

And Montana Central's chief construction engineer said, "Dow! I thought you were one of the others!"

"Me, too," Rowdy acknowledged and released Champion. "Say, you must be the one who fired into Quong's camp!"

"It's a long story," Champion said. "Let's get out of here." He raised his voice a little. "Taisy!"

"Here," the girl answered from somewhere nearby. She shaped up in the gloom. "So you found him."

"Or he found me," Champion said. "Come on, Dow. We've got our horses tied over on the far side of this heap. We crossed over above the slide."

"What is this?" Rowdy asked. "A place where old rocks gather to die?"

"There used to be a mine at the base of Humpback," Champion said. "The Sober Swede they called it. The vein pinched out years and years ago, so I'm told. Then this rock-slide came along and sealed up the shaft."

"Mine?" Rowdy echoed, and he was remembering Doctor Quong telling his crew, ". . . You are about to become miners, my gentle friends. Each and every one of you, . . ." Had Quong some notion of opening the Sober Swede on the chance that it still held gold? The proximity of the Chinaman's camp to the sealed mine indicated that such might be Quong's intentions. But this was no time to discuss the matter, so Rowdy held silent as he clambered after Champion and the girl, who moved haltingly across the face of the slide. In the brush they found the two saddle horses and began leading them, moving through the timber and heading downwards.

Rowdy said, "Feller, you sure came along at the right time."

"It wasn't exactly an accident," Champion explained. "Early this morning, we got word in Tailholt from Avalanche McAllister of last night's raid. I started your partner off to Helena on a special job, and then I headed out to end-of-steel. There McAllister gave me the whole story. That's when I first learned that he'd got a telegram supposedly from me, which made you out an impostor."

"Who do you reckon sent that telegram?"

Champion shrugged. "It could have been anybody. I had several wires written up for the telegrapher the other morning. All somebody would have had to do was slip a fake message in with the rest. Or if the person knew Morse, he could have used the key when the telegrapher wasn't around."

Rowdy said, "That telegram certainly put me in a split stick."

Champion nodded. "When I heard the whole yarn, I started hunting you. I rode on through the canyons, making wide circles, and got to Hatter's just after dark. Taisy told me about your being there and leaving. When I took to the saddle again, she came along. We saw a crew of riders heading towards Humpback. I didn't know you were in the bunch, but those boys just about had to be the crew that had hit the camp. We followed them up the hill. Then we edged towards their fire. That was when I spotted you. You had your hands full."

"That I did," said Rowdy. "And when I got away, you took after me?"

"I was going on guesswork and luck then." Champion conceded. "But we had the start of Quong's men. I saw something moving out on the rock pile. We left the horses, and I went for a look. But when you grabbed me, I thought sure you were the wrong man."

Rowdy said, "Well, we managed to get together. Now if we can get shed of this hill and reach Hatter's. . . ."

They moved on in silence and it wasn't long until they were aware that Quong's crew also had manoeuvred to this far side of the rockslide. Men were here, in the timber; and twice the trio had to haul their horses off into the brush and stand with hands clamped tightly over the nostrils of the mounts while riders went stalking by. At such times Taisy crowded close to the two men, breathing hard. But, with the pursuit moving on past, the three were able to continue their descent, though it took them most of the night. Dawn was beginning to show when they reached the foot of the hill, and a rolling openness lay between them and Hatter's spread.

Champion and Taisy mounted then, and Rowdy swung up behind the construction engineer, the double-burdened cayuse taking this insult with only a perfunctory pitch or two. They moved eastward in the first light, looking often back toward the hill, but pursuit did not materialise; and as the distance broadened, Rowdy began to breathe easier.

"We fooled 'em," he judged.

Against his skin something scratched, and he remembered the spur within his shirt. It had been, he conceded, a pretty good night after all.

13 ⋮ Return to the Ranch

Hatter's place held few happy memories for Rowdy Dow. At this ranch he had nearly been shot by Abner Grubb and had survived only to be ordered from the premises by Taisy, who had hinted, with no noticeable tact, that a bull-whip might be applied to Rowdy's posterior if he didn't move along. But when the log buildings loomed up in the first daylight, Rowdy looked upon the ranch-house with a joyful eye. Hatter hospitality might not have been spelled with a capital H, but after a night on Humpback Hill the place seemed a haven of rest. No fledgling could have returned to its nest with the eagerness which sped Rowdy as he viewed those stout walls.

Mark Champion, though, was showing a certain reluctance as they neared their destination. He said to Taisy, "Mad Hatter was asleep when I stopped by last night. He's probably awake now. Do you suppose he'll allow a railroad man around the place?"

Taisy frowned. "You kept me out all night," she observed. "Likely he'll figger you ought to marry me."

Champion coloured. "I didn't intend—er, I mean I never thought—blast it, no man's going to have to put a shotgun to my back!"

Taisy said tartly, "Don't think I'll be a bit happy about it!"

"Let's not get all fussed up," Rowdy said. "If he won't marry you, I will. Look, Champion, we don't need to worry about what kind of a welcome Hatter will give us. I've got us the passport to his good graces from here on out. Have a squint at this." He delved into his shirt and produced the spur and held it in his hand. It was his own first real look at the object and it glittered in the early sunlight, a silver spur, hand-forged apparently, of Mexican craftsmanship, if Rowdy were any judge. The rowel was large, and the heel-band bore an intricate design, one that Rowdy had never seen before and one which a man seeing would remember. And so at last he looked upon this object which had been sought so persistently by more men than one, looked in fascination, wondering what its secret was. And Mark Champion looked, too, and Taisy.

The girl scowled. "You had it all the time," she accused.

"I got it from a certain Doctor Quong last night. He got it from Miss Arabella. It belongs to Hatter, and it goes back into his hand this morning. Maybe he'll think a mite more highly of railroad men then."

Taisy looked thoughtful. "Maybe I've had you pegged wrong. I reckon you're doing all I could ask."

Champion said, "I hope you've figured Hatter's stand out right, Dow."

"We'll see," said Rowdy and tucked the spur back inside his shirt.

They rode into the ranch yard less than an hour later and swung down from their horses at the corrals. The bunk-house had stirred to life, but such of the crew as loitered in the yard gave them only curious stares; the presence of Taisy lent assurance that these strangers had a right to be here. They came past the watering trough where Rowdy had immersed Abner Grubb the day before, and they climbed the gallery steps and entered the ranch-house. And there, in the living-room, sat Abner Grubb.

Rowdy instantly took a sideward step, his hand falling towards his hip; he had underestimated this long-faced banker once and had been caught flat-footed; he was not making that mistake twice. But Grubb raised a placating hand. "Take it easy, Dow," he said. "I have no quarrel with you."

"When," asked Rowdy, "did *you* get religion?"

Grubb said, "I only knew what Avalanche McAllister told me when I came out to end-of-steel yesterday morning. It looked bad for you, Dow. And when I first saw you in Quong's camp last night, I was even surer that McAllister had you pegged right. But when they all lit on you and you made your fight, I realised that you were working for the railroad in your own fashion. I faded away and threw a few bullets. Possibly it helped."

Rowdy squinted an eye thoughtfully. "It listens good," he said. "But how did you know where to find Quong's camp?"

"I trailed his men there."

Rowdy's brows rose. "The range was positively cluttered last night," he observed. "You had nerve, walking into Quong's camp and trying to do business with him."

"I've known him slightly for many years. This isn't the first time he's been around this part of the country. He's always posed as a palaeontologist, but I have had reason to think him a scoundrel. I knew he'd listen to money talk."

"And you really hoped to buy the spur?"

"To turn it over to Hatter. I'll confess that I intended using it as a bargaining point to get railroad right of way. Maybe I foresaw a possibility of lining my own pockets—in a legitimate way. That's no sin, Dow. You got the spur?"

"I got it," Rowdy said, "but me, I'm on the payroll."

Mad Hatter said, "What is all this?"

He stood in the doorway of his bedroom where he had materialised so unobtrusively that every person in the room started. He stood, running his hand through his silvery grey mane, his eyes shuttling from one visitor to another. He scowled as he glanced at Champion; and Taisy tensed herself, apparently fearful of the explosiveness that sometimes ruled this tortured man. He scowled at Rowdy, and Rowdy reached inside his shirt and produced the spur and held it forth.

"I believe," said Rowdy, "that this is your property."

Hatter took the spur and turned it over and over in his hands, staring at it blankly at first, and then his expression became intent, and he seemed lost from the rest of them, a man deep in some thought maze. His mouth twitched at the corners, the wrinkles deepened between his eyebrows. He placed the spur against his heel as if determining how well it fitted; he scowled. Then, without a word, he retreated into his bedroom, closing the door behind him.

Rowdy let out his breath in a long sigh, a small explosion in the piled-up silence. He said, "I could use some breakfast."

It broke the spell. Taisy stirred herself. "I'll fix some vittles," she said.

Shortly thereafter they sat down to table, Grubb, Champion, Rowdy and Taisy; and when they'd eaten, Taisy disappeared, going into Hatter's bedroom and returning not many minutes later. She looked scared. "He ain't saying nothing," she reported. "He's just walking the floor, holding that spur in his hand. I hope he isn't getting one of his spells."

They filed back into the big front room where Rowdy had whiled away an aimless afternoon the day before, and they took chairs and fumbled with the stockman's journals and held their silence. From the bedroom beyond, they could hear the steady pacing of Hatter; his boots beat a slow, measured cadence against the floor, back and forth, back and forth. His tread became a nerve-racking monotony, like the endless dripping of water. It went on as one hour followed another, and it took its toll of the listeners.

At last Champion looked at his watch. "I should be getting back to camp. But I'd like to talk to him before I go."

Taisy shook her head. "Leave him be."

Champion said thoughtfully, "I could take a bunch of

the terriers up Humpback Hill and clean out that snakes' nest." His voice turned futile. "But likely Quong's moved camp by now. Confound it, I'm useless!"

Grubb said, "If you have to get along, maybe I could dicker with Hatter when he gets in a mood to listen."

Champion said, "I'll wait a while longer."

Rowdy glanced towards the bedroom. "That spur means something to him," he judged. "He's trying to puzzle it out. I've got a feeling, gents, that we'll have the answer to everything when Hatter walks out of there."

But the day was to drag on without Mad Hatter putting in an appearance, and the tension grew in this house until it was a suffocating thing. In Rowdy, always a restive soul, was an urge to be out and doing, yet he was held here as surely as though he were chained, held by a desire to know what went on in that sick mind in the room beyond. And the same compelling need that gripped him was gripping the others, he could tell. Champion sat fixedly in a chair, his hands clasped, his eyes sombre. Grubb, the most fidgety of the group, wandered aimlessly from the room to the gallery; he moved from one chair to another and plucked at magazines and discarded them. Sometimes Rowdy dozed, as did the others, for none of them had slept the night before.

When at long last the dusk came and Taisy went about lighting the lamps, still nothing had changed; still the four waited while Hatter paced endlessly; and then Taisy said, "I'll get supper."

"We could go out to the cook-shack and eat with the boys," Champion said gallantly.

"I want something to do," Taisy retorted, an edge to her voice.

Rowdy knew how she felt. Given the materials, he could have braided a reata that long day. Taisy disappeared towards the kitchen; stove lids clattered and a sink pump creaked and soon the odour of frying steak permeated the house; and Rowdy realised that he was very hungry. He rubbed a hand over his chin; he could have used a shave. In due course, Taisy called them to table, and again the group gathered in the kitchen.

"I'll see if *he*'ll eat something," Taisy said a little later and went towards Hatter's bedroom.

When she returned, she looked less strained. "He wants all of you to stay," she said. "He's been piecing things together in his mind. He says he'll have something to tell you soon." Her face puckered. "It's been a terrible day for him. He looks like he's been wrestling with the devil."

But when they returned to the big room, Mad Hatter still kept himself aloof, and his boots still beat that steady cadence on his bedroom floor. An hour passed while they waited; Champion took to prowling the room; Taisy maintained a stony face but Rowdy saw that her hands were often locked together and her fingers twitched. Grubb dug a cigar case from an inner coat pocket and offered the weed around and was refused. He put a cheroot between his teeth, scraped away with a match, thought better of the act, and walked out to the gallery. The odour of the cigar reached back into the room through the partially opened door.

Rowdy felt like yawning and couldn't manage it. He had a hunch that if anybody were to touch him he would twang like a guitar string.

And then, suddenly, the long waiting was done, the long nothingness was ended; but the manner in which this came to pass was completely unexpected. A gun barked, and Rowdy was sure that he rose three feet out of his chair. Gun-thunder rolled again and again, and Rowdy was simultaneously aware of several things. Abner Grubb was shooting, out there on the gallery; and Grubb was calling frantically. And in Mad Hatter's bedroom the pacing had ceased and a big man had fallen.

Rowdy rushed first to the front door, getting there at the same time as Mark Champion, and the shoulders of the two wedged as they tried to force through. Rowdy got past, in time to glimpse Grubb vaulting the railing of the gallery and sprinting off into the dark. Grubb paused, looking back and beckoning to them to follow. "Quong!" the banker shouted. "He's out here somewhere!"

Champion groaned. "We should have known! We should have guessed that that sneaking devil wouldn't give up the spur just because you got off Humpback with it!"

Rowdy said, "You help Grubb."

Turning, Rowdy dashed back into the house. He came through the living-room and put his hand to the door of Hatter's bedroom, praying that it wouldn't be locked; and he burst inside to find Hatter sprawled upon the floor. The man was unconscious, his silvery mane matted with blood. Taisy, at Rowdy's elbow looked towards the window. There was a small neat hole in it.

"Give me a hand!" Rowdy panted. "We'll get him to the bed!"

Between the two of them they lifted him; the strength of desperation was in Rowdy. They got a pillow under Hatter's head, and Rowdy put his ear to the man's chest and said, "He's still alive. Quick, we'll need hot water and bandages."

Taisy said, "He's still got the spur in his hand."

Rowdy looked. "That's right. Thank heavens Grubb was out there on the gallery and could move fast after that first shot! Quong didn't have time to get through the window. It was the spur Quong wanted."

Taisy said, "Look! His eyelids are fluttering!"

Mad Hatter's eyes opened, but they were glazed and there was no intelligence in them. Yet Rowdy knew this moment might count for everything and he bent close to the man. "The spur?" Rowdy demanded. "What makes it valuable, Hatter? You've got to tell us!"

Hatter's lips moved, only the ghost of sound coming

from them. Then his eyes had closed again, and Rowdy wasn't sure there was life in the man.

"What did he say?" Taisy asked breathlessly.

Rowdy shook his head. "It certainly didn't make sense. It sounded as if he said, 'The Sober Swede.'"

Taisy hurried from the room to fetch hot water and cloths for bandages, and Rowdy stood looking down upon the unconscious Hatter, a hundred questions whirling through his mind. The Sober Swede——? His cherubic face knotted in bewilderment, he felt as mixed-up as a mouse in a mandolin by the time Taisy returned. Together they began ministering to Hatter's hurt. Rowdy swabbed at the wound, while Taisy tore a sheet into strips. The bushwhacker's bullet had creased Hatter's head, leaving a bloody furrow not far from the scar that marked his old wound. While Rowdy's nimble fingers worked, his mind was still busy.

"The Sober Swede . . ." he mused. "That's the name of the mine Champion mentioned, the old mine at the base of Humpback. Where the rockslide sealed up the shaft."

"That's the place," Taisy said. She worked with a cool carefulness as though Mad Hatter were no more than a side of beef, but Rowdy noticed she was holding her lips tight to keep from crying.

"Hmmm," Rowdy murmured. "Maybe the vein didn't pinch out after all. The spur's tied up with the mine somehow. And Quong wanted the spur enough to risk coming right into the ranch yard."

Taisy shook her head. "You're gnawin' at the wrong hitch-rail, mister. The Sober Swede played out before I was born, but I've heard the story a heap of times. That mine was never worth nothing. A couple of schemers sold it to a drunk Swede years back. When the Swede inspected his property and saw how bad he'd been swindled, he sobered up pronto. That's how the mine got its name. The Swede cleared out of the country. That mine was anybody's for the taking for quite a spell afterwards, but nobody wanted it. It wasn't worth their time. Then the slide closed it up."

Abner Grubb loomed in the bedroom doorway, Mark Champion crowding close behind him. "That's absolutely right, Taisy," the banker said. He turned his gimlet-eyed look upon the still form of Hatter. "How is he?"

"Hard bit," Rowdy said. "You get Quong?"

Mark Champion spoke. "Looks like he got clear away. He must have come alone, and he moved fast and quietly. The shots fetched the crew from the bunk-house and they're still looking. We turned back to see how much damage he'd done."

Taisy had fastened a pad and tie, and, with Rowdy's help, was covering the wound. She said woodenly, "We have to get him to a doctor. To-night!"

"And the nearest one's at Tailholt," Mark Champion said with a groan.

"He could be moved by wagon to end-of-steel," Grubb observed. "A train could carry him on into town."

"I don't care how it's done," Taisy said. "Just so's it's done fast."

Thus it was decided, and Champion went out to see to harnessing up a team, and Taisy shortly followed him. Rowdy stretched himself, feeling taut after his labours, and looked grimly at Grubb.

"It's been a bad night," Rowdy observed, but he didn't put all his bitterness into words. He'd waited through a long day, hoping at last to learn the secret of the phantom spur; and he'd been on the verge of hearing that secret when a bushwhacker's bullet had closed Hatter's mouth. Moreover, the man lay badly injured, perhaps dying; and there was a drastic need to move him to the construction camp. Quong might have come here alone, but Pocatello and the other railroad raiders were probably lurking not far away; so danger might well ride with Hatter's entourage through every mile of the canyons.

The same thought seemed to be in Abner Grubb, for the banker said, "We could take Hatter's crew along with us. We'd make a pretty sizable force."

Rowdy shook his head. "The ranch can't be left unguarded," he said. He was remembering Pocatello's temptation of the night before, when the straw boss of the raiders had considered sprinkling this place with bullets. He began pacing. "I wonder how they're coming with that wagon."

"What was this talk about the Sober Swede?" Grubb asked.

"Hatter stayed conscious just long enough to mention the mine."

"Strange!" Grubb reflected. "Why should he have done that?"

Rowdy shrugged. "We'll have to ask Doctor Quong."

He left the house and came around it towards the barn, mindful that the darkness might well be dangerous, mindful that Quong could still be lingering close. Some of the crew had given up the search, for men drifted into the yard. Rowdy moved as a shadow moves, and he saw that a light wagon had been wheeled from a shed and a team hitched to it. Champion was working by lantern-light. With this beacon to draw him, Rowdy came quietly to where Champion and Taisy stood. They were very close to each other. Rowdy didn't mean to be an eavesdropper, but suddenly he again found himself in that rôle.

Champion was saying intently, "I don't want to be cruel or to distress you at a time like this, Taisy. But it's got to be faced. Whether he dies or gets better, you'll be left here alone—at least for a while."

"I'm coming along with him," Taisy said stoutly.

"I was thinking about your situation in the days ahead," Champion said, his voice softening. "You know how I feel about you. You haven't given me much encouragement, but I love you, Taisy. Marry me when we get to Tailholt. Let me be the one to take care of you."

Rowdy, stepping into the rim of lantern-light, coughed discreetly. "We'd better get started for camp," he said.

Taisy whirled, facing him, a picture of wild splendour in this dim light, her long black hair tumbled to her shoulders, her pretty face twisted with a hopeless sort of anguish. "Tell him!" she said to Rowdy. "Tell him why I can't marry him. You know the truth. I'm not really Hatter's girl. Tell him that my father was a thief! And it was just yesterday that Abner said I was something like him!"

Rowdy came forward and put his arms around her gently, feeling her body tremble. He said, "There's been too much of too much for you lately, lady. Come along, now; we've got to get your dad moved."

This broke the spell; Taisy stiffened, then took herself out of Rowdy's arms. "You're right," she said. She got her bull whip from the shed, climbed to the wagon seat, took the reins and drove the team to the front of the gallery.

At Rowdy's suggestion they fetched a mattress and placed it in the wagon box. It took all three men to move Hatter, and while Champion, Grubb and Rowdy toiled at this, Taisy hurried with blankets to make the softest possible bed for the wounded man. When they had Hatter laid upon it, Rowdy prised the spur from Hatter's hand and gave it to Champion.

"You take charge of this," Rowdy said. "If the railroad has a safe in its office, you'd better put it there."

Champion said, "Nobody will get it away from me. You can be mighty sure of that."

Grubb said, "I'll be riding along with you."

"And me," Rowdy said. He looked off into the darkness; his real wish was to take the trail of Quong, but the greater need was here, with the wagon. "I'll have to borrow a horse again."

"I forgot to tell you," Taisy said. "That one you had

last night came home this afternoon. Some of the crew found it standing at the corral gate."

Rowdy nodded. "Then Quong's outfit cleared off Humpback and didn't bother taking the spare horse along." He glanced at Champion. "No use bringing any of your crew here. Our pigeons have flown."

Taisy said, "You can ride on the wagon seat with me."

Champion murmured something about taking the reins, but Taisy pointed out that she knew the terrain better. She sent the bull whip flicking above the horses' ears; and the wagon went rumbling across the yard, Rowdy perched on the seat beside Taisy, while Grubb and Champion up in saddles, flanked the wagon on either side. No further suggestion was made that Hatter's crew accompany them, and soon the darkness swallowed wagon and riders; and Rowdy, looking back, saw the lights of the ranch grow smaller.

There was a road which Taisy followed, and it brought them by easy stages across the rolling country and up the rimrock ridge into the canyons. Now they were completely pocketed in darkness, and Rowdy was glad indeed for Taisy's knowledge of this land. On either side, canyon walls reared, the rumbling of the wagon and the clip-clop of shod hooves upon rock stirring up a thousand echoes; and Rowdy grew more and more mindful that an ambush might be laid anywhere along this road.

Apparently the same thought crossed Mark Champion's mind, for the construction engineer jogged his horse on up ahead and was soon lost to sight. For many miles Champion often vanished into the darkness, only to ride back to the wagon from time to time. Thus he gave them tacit assurance that the trail ahead was clear. Rowdy, as jumpy as a frog in a frying pan, was grateful for Champion's scouting.

Taisy handed the reins to Rowdy several times; and on these occasions she climbed back into the wagon bed and tarried a while with Mad Hatter, returning wordlessly to the seat each time. Finally she said, "He's still unconscious." After a while she began crying so silently that only the trembling of her shoulder, pressed against Rowdy's, told him of her grief. He wanted mightily to put his arm around her and comfort her, did Rowdy; but there was another man for whom such work was more obviously cut out.

"I'll change off with you for a while," Rowdy said, the next time Champion rode back to the wagon.

The construction engineer stepped down from saddle, and Rowdy swung up to the leather, feeling like the little chap with the bare belly and the bow and arrows. It was probably the first time Cupid needed a shave! With Champion on the wagon seat beside Taisy, Rowdy went scouting ahead. A quarter of a mile onward, Rowdy paused, sitting his saddle and scanning the canyon walls on either side, listening intently the while. No sound broke the silence but the distant rumbling of the wagon. Turning back to meet it, Rowdy let himself be seen.

And so they moved through the long night, and sometimes Rowdy dozed in the saddle, for he hadn't caught up on his sleep. Not by a jugful! These canyons were monotonously alike, and moving through them was like moving upon a treadmill; a fellow kept himself going, but he didn't seem to get anywhere. The wagon could progress only at a snail's pace, lest Hatter be jarred unnecessarily, and Rowdy had to match his speed to Taisy's. Then, when the night was far gone, the canyons grew broader, and Rowdy sensed a familiarity that made him look for landmarks.

Riding back to the wagon, he said, "We can't be far from the construction camp. In fact, I'd bet next month's pay that this is the canyon where I ran into that big brute with the horny back night before last."

Champion's voice was tinged with surprise. "You saw the dinosaur? I wanted to ask you about that to-day, but you were dozing when it crossed my mind."

"I saw the critter," Rowdy said grimly.

"So did McAllister and a lot of the Chinese," Champion said. "But nobody seemed to have got very close to it. I'd like to hear more about it, Dow. I just can't make myself believe that there are actually prehistoric beasts roaming this country. I've tried to argue that it's some sort of hallucination. Yet all the descriptions jibe."

Rowdy said, "It seemed like a dream when I thought about it in broad daylight." But even as he spoke, he felt again a touch of that weirdness that had gripped him when his horse had bolted through the storm towards that lumbering, ungainly thing he'd glimpsed so briefly. He shook his head, dispelling the memory. "I'm going to scout around some more," he announced.

For suddenly it had come to Rowdy that if there had indeed been a dinosaur in this canyon the huge creature must have left tracks! That was so obvious that it hadn't crossed his mind till now. And suddenly he wanted to prove to himself that there were no tracks. Jogging the horse, he left the wagon once more, but this time, instead of scanning the roadside for possible places of ambush, he tried recalling his wild ride of two nights ago. Yonder, to the south-east, he guessed, lay the construction camp. He'd had his back to the camp the other night; so now he went riding back along the canyon, heading to the northwest. After a while he dismounted, scraped a match aglow, and had a look around.

In places a thin layer of silt covered the canyon's rocky floor, and in this dirt he could plainly see the hoofprints made by the horse he was riding to-night. Then he muttered at the futility of this quest. Senseless as trying to light a match on a bar of soap! The rain would have washed away any tracks of the other night!

Still Rowdy pursued his search. After all, if a dinosaur indeed roamed these canyons—and Rowdy had seen one with his own eyes!—then the huge monster was still hereabouts and would still be leaving tracks. Thinking thus, Rowdy again felt the short hairs rise at the nape of his neck, and he was unashamed of an impulse to pile upon Champion's horse and head back to the wagon. Instead, he rode onward, stopping from time to time to dismount and light matches and have a look at the ground. Sometimes the floor was rocky—too rocky to show any kind of print. But Rowdy persisted, torn by a desire to find the tracks he sought—and by a greater desire *not* to find them!

And then they were there, in the light of a match, a mile or two farther up the canyon than where he was sure he'd seen the dinosaur the other night. They were there, in the sandy carpeting of the canyon floor—huge, five-toed tracks, larger than any Rowdy had ever seen before. Spaced out as they were, they gave him an all too graphic idea of the size of the monster that had made them.

He remembered the Chinese shrieking their terror in the night. He remembered his own panic, and the sweat came out on him now. The match burned down to his fingers, and he groped his way into the saddle and wheeled the horse about and rode at a hard tilt until reason restored itself. Then he sat his saddle and listened for the rumbling of the wagon; and having oriented himself by the sound, he headed towards the wagon and drew abreast of it with a sensation of relief.

"Champion," he said. "If that dragon that stampeded the Chinks is a dream, it's the only dream that ever left tracks! I've just seen them."

15 : The Dangerous Dark

They came to end-of-steel in due course; and Rowdy, at first puzzled as to why the yellow welt of the grade ran so much farther, realised that almost a mile of track had been laid in the two days since he'd quit the construction camp. The camp had hop-skipped after the steel, lifting itself by its boot straps and moving along the canyon with the meandering rails. It was still in the throes of settling, and the sea of tents and rough shacks looked as if it had been stirred by a gigantic egg beater. But Rowdy lifted his chest in a heartfelt sigh of relief at sight of journey's end. In spite of his fears they had come through unscathed.

But where, then, was Doctor Quong?

Rowdy thought he knew, but his immediate concern was still for Mad Hatter. The man lay unconscious in the wagon bed, and the rough ride had doubtless done him no good. But now they were among friends, and the resources of Montana Central could be put to caring for Hatter. Friends? Rowdy swung down from Mark Champion's saddle to find a heavy hand clamping upon his shoulder and a set of whiskers tickling his ear.

"Hoots, mon!" roared the voice of Avalanche McAllister. "So ye have the nerve to show your-r face again. 'Tis a taste of my fist I'll be gieing ye!"

The whiskered Scot lifted Rowdy from the ground and began dancing him; but Champion said sharply, "McAllister! I told you day before yesterday that that telegram was a fake!"

McAllister released Rowdy, the Scot's big, red face

showing regret. " 'Twas the sight o'him that r-reminded me of all my troubles."

"We've all been mistaken about him," said Abner Grubb, coming down off his horse. "He's for Montana Central, all right. I saw him in action, McAllister."

A wave of excitement had swept the camp with the coming of the wagon, sleepy-eyed workers tumbling from tents; and now a car on a siding began disgorging people in various stages of dress. Among them was the huge form of Bartholomew B. Bartholomew, and the diminutive one of little Launcelot, clad in an embroidered nightgown; and Miss Arabella Hatter appeared, too, a robe clutched tightly about her. But it was Stumpy Grampis, his pants pulled hastily on and his hair tousled, who caught Rowdy's eye.

"How's the world using you, partner?" Rowdy cried, extending his hand.

"It ain't to be put into words with ladies present," said Stumpy.

"Mr. Grampis has been sulking ever since a recent trip to Helena," little Launcelot remarked. "We just got back this evening."

Grubb and Champion meanwhile were explaining about Mad Hatter, and Miss Arabella climbed gingerly into the wagon to have a look at her stricken cousin. In the babble of talk, Bartholomew B. Bartholomew's voice suddenly rose louder than the rest. There was a crying need for leadership here, and B. B. was willing to rise to the occasion. "Never mind the rest of it," he shouted. "The important thing is to get this wounded man to a doctor at once. Is there a competent one in Tailholt?"

"Yes," said Taisy. "If it's a sick horse that needs tending to."

"Champion, we'll wire Helena at once," B. B. bellowed. "We'll have their best doctor start to Tailholt. Meanwhile, we'll put this poor unfortunate man aboard my own car and have a special engine take it to Tailholt at once. I tell you, we'll move heaven and earth to show that Montana Central, far from being a soulless corporation, has the heart of the Samaritan."

"You wouldn't be remembering that you need right of way across Hatter's place, now would you, *pater*?" asked little Launcelot.

"Quiet!" B. B. roared. "Some of you men, lend a hand to move Mr. Hatter to my private car."

Miss Arabella clambered from the wagon and began supervising matters. Rowdy stepped towards her. "I thought you'd like to know," he said, "that we've found your spur for you. Champion has it."

"That's splendid," said Miss Hatter. "I just couldn't face Cousin Lucius without it, you know. But I grew so weary of Tailholt. I asked Mr. Bartholomew to bring me out to end-of-steel on an inspection trip he was making. And most fortunate for the stockholders that I came! Do you know that inefficiency is rampant on this project? I've made a list of seventy-six suggestions for Mr. Champion."

"He'll appreciate that no end," said Rowdy solemnly. "Fact is, he'll be as happy as if he were shoeing a centipede."

"Shooing a centipede?" Miss Hatter looked puzzled. "Now why should the poor man take pleasure in that?"

Taisy had climbed down from the wagon and was moving after the group which was carefully carrying her foster father to B. B.'s private car. The girl's walk was unsteady, the only outward manifestation of how gruelling this night had been. B. B. heaved his big bulk everywhere, shouting orders. The telegrapher's key soon was rattling; word went winging to Helena that would fetch a doctor; a locomotive was being detached from a string of flats and backed to Bartholomew's own car.

Rowdy found Stumpy hovering near him. "Been earning your pay, old hoss?" Rowdy asked.

"At least we got a new batch o' coolies to replace

them that hit the grit when the dinosaur walked the other night," Stumpy said sullenly. "Rowdy, what is the State law regarding a feller of my size ambushin' a feller little Launcelot's size?"

"You recruited more Chinks, Stumpy? How?"

"Hop Gow."

"Champion said you'd gone to Helena to do a job. How is old Hop?"

"I didn't get much of a chance to talk to him," Stumpy said sourly, then brightened. "But I got to ask him about Doctor Quong. Figgered one Chinaman might have a line on another. You ever see Hop Gow fighting mad, Rowdy? Quong's a renegade Chink who used to be a hatchetman for the Suey Sing tong in Frisco. But he sold out his tong when he got in a tight, and half a dozen *boo how doy* got killed on account of Quong's double-cross. The Suey Sings are Hop Gow's tong, and Quong ain't popular with the other tongs, either. The Six Companies have got a price on his head, too. There won't be no wailing in Chinatown when Quong gets gathered to his ancestors."

"Hmmm," Rowdy said. "He was a hired killer to start with, eh? Stumpy, I want you to go into Tailholt with Mad Hatter. And I want you to stick close to him till he's in a doctor's hands."

"You figger Quong's after him?"

"Quong's after something; I'm not sure yet what it is. There's a sealed mine at the base of Humpback—the Sober Swede, they call it. Me, I'm a million years behind on my sleep and I'm going to do a little catching up. Then I'm going back to Humpback. Once you've got Hatter safe to Tailholt, you can look for men at the mine. Meanwhile I'll feel better if one of us is riding with Hatter."

Stumpy gave his pants a hitch. "I'm your huckleberry."

Abner Grubb stood nearby. "I might as well be going into Tailholt myself," the banker said. "Grampis and I can both keep an eye out for Quong. But I still can't see why Quong should be interested in the Sober Swede. You'll be wasting your time, Dow! I assure you, that mine is absolutely worthless."

"Maybe so," said Rowdy.

Hatter had been loaded into Bartholomew's car; and it had been decided that Taisy, Mark Champion, Abner Grubb, Stumpy and the Bartholomews, senior and junior, would be going into town with the wounded man. Just what Miss Arabella Hatter, that self-appointed efficiency expert, had elected to do Rowdy didn't learn, nor was he interested. He wanted a place to sleep, and the telegrapher offered to provide him with a bunk. Rowdy groped to it, stripped off his boots, loosened his belt, and was fast asleep within five minutes of the time he'd stretched himself out.

Not even the clamour of construction all around him roused him: he slept himself out, and it was near noon when he came forth. A shave and a hearty breakfast made him feel better; and he sought out Avalanche McAllister, who was supervising the track-laying, and asked for the loan of a horse.

McAllister squinted sceptically; it was obvious that the giant's suspicions died hard. "Champion's mount is still here," growled the Scot. " 'Tis na use for it he has at the moment."

"I admire your fine spirit of co-operation," said Rowdy, and went to get the horse.

Shortly thereafter he was picking his way out of camp, moving among the myriad Irish workers and the lately-recruited Chinese. Hop Gow was sending coolies in by each train that came to end-of-steel, Rowdy learned, and McAllister was sweating to teach these raw workmen the rudiments of railroad building.

The camp behind him, Rowdy threaded through the canyons, moving in a general north-westerly direction; but soon he found the road over which Taisy had tooled the wagon last night, and he followed this road towards Hatter's ranch. These canyons were not quite the undecipherable maze they had once been to him; he had traversed them enough times now to have fixed certain landmarks in his mind, and he rode along with his eyes alert. Where were those railroad raiders? But peace dwelt in the canyons; a hawk wheeled overhead in an ominously cloudy sky, and rodents scurried among the rocks, rattling their claws.

It might rain before another day was past, Rowdy reflected, and thought of the dinosaur that stalked in storm.

Nearing the place where he'd cached the saddle he'd taken from the raider's horse that stormy night, he sought out the kak and packed it along. He rode down off the rimrock ridge in mid-afternoon, passing the place where he'd been caught up by Quong's men, and came across the rolling terrain towards Hatter's ranch. He found the crew about the place and he made a brief report to them, helped himself to food, left the spare saddle at the ranch, and then took to riding again.

Now he had his eye fixed on Humpback Hill and he rode steadily towards it but kept his horse at a walk. He preferred darkness to cloak his reconnaissance, and this gave him time to kill. But he was always alert. The enemy had to be one place or another, and he was glad he'd sent Stumpy back to Tailholt with Hatter. But the only movement Rowdy saw was that of grazing cattle which bore Hatter's brand; and as the dusk gathered, he found himself at the wooded base of the great hill.

He'd had a lot of time for thinking to-day, had Rowdy, but nothing had come of it that he could wrap up in a neat package and tie with a blue ribbon. Yet he felt himself close to the core of a mystery and some instinct had clamoured ever since last night that the answer was the Sober Swede. Now he made a simple, fireless supper, delving into his saddlebag for food he'd stored when he'd stopped at Hatter's. Having eaten, he began cautiously to skirt the base of Humpback, heading to where that rock-slide had moved down the hill and sealed the entrance to the old mine.

There was still light enough for him to see his way, and before long he heard sounds ahead—sounds he found difficult to interpret. Thereafter Rowdy came down from his saddle and led the horse, and it was not long before he found himself in the shadow of the dump heap of the original excavation. From the size of this dump heap, Rowdy judged that the shaft had been run in straight under the slope for a considerable distance—fifty yards or more. Nearby was a shack, rotted and tumbled-down; and behind this, Rowdy tied his horse. Now he slipped forward on foot, and soon he had a view of where the opening of the mine had been.

And here he found Doctor Quong.

The man was alone, and he would have made the busiest beaver seem like a slothful sluggard with the sleeping sickness. For Quong had felled and trimmed three small trees and made of these a tripod from which he had suspended a pulley block and tackle, and with this device he had obviously spent a hard day at hoisting away the larger boulders which clogged the mine entrance. It was almost too dark for Quong to work, but still he persisted, for he had moved most of the rocks and thus had nearly unsealed the mine. As Rowdy watched, Quong picked up a shovel and attacked loose gravel and smaller rocks, then returned to the tripod to struggle with another large boulder.

Rowdy sucked in a long hard breath. The night before last, Quong had proposed that his railroad raiders be put to such a task, but now Quong was working alone, looking not at all his usual dapper self. Where then were Pocatello and the others? Rowdy could make a guess, and he was once again glad that he had commissioned Stumpy to accompany Hatter. Or had Quong had a change of heart and decided to open the mine alone, keeping its contents for himself only?

In either case, Rowdy was just as interested as to what lay inside that clogged shaft as was Quong; but he guessed that Quong wouldn't welcome any offer of help. Therefore Rowdy hugged the shadows, watching Quong toil and taking a chuckling pleasure in the thought that he, too, would enjoy the fruits of Quong's labours. And then he saw that Quong was clambering over the last of the litter and squeezing himself into the opening he had made.

The Chinese having vanished from sight, Rowdy was instantly stealing forward. He sent a little gravel rolling as he clambered towards the opening; and suddenly mindful that silence might literally be golden in this case, he paused, hauled off his boots, and left them lying. Climbing onward in his stockinged feet, he came to the mine entrance and peered inside. Only blackness lay beyond—blackness and silence. But as Rowdy paused, he heard soft movement in those dark depths.

Quong, who seemed to have prepared himself in all other respects—as witness the block and tackle and the shovel—had apparently fetched neither candle nor lantern; but Rowdy was glad of this. He squeezed his shoulders into the opening Quong had made and had a bad moment as the realisation smote him that he might be briefly silhouetted against such light as remained and therefore visible if Quong chanced to be glancing backward. Then Rowdy was inside the shaft and moving forward on hands and knees. He essayed standing and found that he could; and he paused then in the stifling dark, his ears straining. No longer did he hear Quong's slight movement up ahead of him.

But Quong was here. For Quong said out of the darkness, "Please to stand where you are. A gun is in my hand and my finger is on the trigger. You were clumsy on the rockpile outside, and I have been awaiting you. This is a big mine, but not big enough for two, I am afraid."

Again Rowdy sucked in a long hard breath, and a feeling of bitterness smote him. He had been too eager, and this was what his eagerness had cost him.

16 : That Thirsty Lamb

Stumpy Grampis came to Tailholt in the first flush of dawn, at the hour when Rowdy, bedded down in the telegrapher's bunk, was getting in his best licks. But for Stumpy there'd been a broken night, and he was as peevish as a porcupine with ingrown quills. It might have been different if the train which had borne the unconscious Mad Hatter to town had been beset by Quong's minions. Stumpy fancied himself as quite a repeller of boarders, but as it was he'd had nothing to do but twiddle his thumbs over the unballasted miles. Confound it, there was no more justice in the world than there was juice in a boiled boot! Stumpy felt plumb stepped on.

Nor did circumstance supply him with any position of prime importance when the locomotive hauling Bartholomew's private car wheezed into Tailholt. There were more than enough hands to bear the wounded Hatter to soft bedding in the Traveller's Rest; and Stumpy, the smallest man in the group, got elbowed out of the way. The doctor, summoned from Helena, had not yet arrived, but Bartholomew, who'd become as concerned over Hatter as though the man were a gilt-edged investment—which indeed he was!—made the wires hot again and learned that the medico was en route. By the time Stumpy had breakfasted and wandered dismally back to the hotel, the doctor had come.

"Well, well," said the doctor, rubbing his hands, "what have we here?" But he was looking at Hatter, not at Stumpy.

The sawbones, a plump, fussy fellow who smelled of liniment, made his examination while Grubb, Champion, Taisy, B. B., little Launcelot and Stumpy watched in silence. The doctor bent over the bed for a long time, examining Hatter's scalp as carefully as though he were looking for animal life, then stroked his jowls thoughtfully, contemplated his feet and the ceiling of the room, and spoke. "The recent wound is nothing alarming. But he has an old wound which interests me. It, too, is a bullet wound. I dare say there is pressure on the brain as a result of it. Has this man been subject to erratic spells? Forgetfulness? So——! An operation is required here. A very delicate operation. . . ." He looked around, his eyebrows rising.

Taisy said, "You go ahead and do it, Doc."

Champion moved close and put an arm around her; Taisy stood numbly, not protesting, not moving.

"Clear out of here, all of you," the doctor ordered. "I've fetched my nurse with me. She'll be here as soon as she's had breakfast. I'll operate at once."

He shooed them out of the room as though they were a swarm of flies; and into the hallway of the hotel, the group disbanded to go their separate ways. Stumpy clomped back to the street, feeling as useless as a bottomless bucket. He could, he supposed, head back to end-of-steel. Rowdy had told him to stick close to Hatter until the man was in the doctor's hands. Quong's crew would surely not have the nerve to make a play against Hatter in Tailholt. Stumpy wasn't needed any more than a handful of gravel was needed in a shoe.

Where was it Rowdy had said he was going? Some closed mine at the foot of Humpback called the Sober Swede. Crazy name for a mine! Why not the Drunken Dutchman? Now there was a name to fire the imagination! Or the 'Orry-eyed 'Ungarian? Or the Tanked Turk?

It came to Stumpy that it had been a long time between drinks.

Moreover, if ever a man was entitled to a short snort,

it was Gabriel Q. Grampis. Hadn't he promised himself one the first night he'd come to Tailholt? And hadn't he been circumvented by a series of events that had totalled up to a round goose egg, so far as achievement was concerned? Dang it all, a man needed bolstering when destiny did nothing to enliven existence! And he was off duty, wasn't he? Come to think of it, he'd been off duty most of the time since he'd taken this railroad job!

Stopping a passing grader, Stumpy learned that it would be an hour or so before a work-train left for end-of-steel. Whereupon Stumpy bow-legged into the nearest saloon—which happened to be the one from whence Doctor Quong had fired a shot across the street into the Odd Fellows building. Bellying up to the bar, Stumpy got the eye of the indolent barkeep who had proved to be such a dehydrated font of knowledge at the time of their previous meeting. This worthy inspected Stumpy with considerable disdain. "What'll it be?" the apron inquired.

"A drink," said Stumpy.

The apron reached for a pitcher and poured a full glass, but Stumpy was too preoccupied with his woes to notice this unorthodox procedure. Hoisting the glass, Stumpy took a good swallow and instantly sprayed it out across the bar. *"Phuft!"* Stumpy gasped, spluttering wildly. "What in tarnation is this stuff?"

"Lemonade," said the barkeep.

"Lemonade! I said I wanted a *drink*!"

"Ain't you heard?" said the barkeep. "That big-bellied railroad official, the one from Chicago, ordered all the saloons to quit selling the hard stuff. Said he'd keep the railroad trade out of here if we didn't. It's a sad situation, mister."

By now Stumpy was recalling Miss Arabella Hatter's crusade against the saloons and Bartholomew B. Bartholomew's ill-advised promise to back the spinster in her catastrophic campaign. A Blue Ribbon town this had turned out to be! Stumpy felt lower than caterpillar tracks in a wagon rut. "Ain't there a drop of real drinking to be had?" he implored.

The barkeep shook his head. "Just one exception, mister. Snakebite."

Stumpy brightened. "You got a snake handy?"

"Not me," said the barkeep. "Heard tell some jigger brought a Diamondback into town last night. Fellers stood in a line half a mile long waiting their turn to get bit. Maybe you could get in the line."

"Not a chance," said Stumpy, for he was thinking that with this kind of luck that rattler would doubtless be too tired to lift its head by the time Stumpy's turn came to be bitten.

The barkeep filled Stumpy's glass with lemonade. "The stuff ain't too bad if you hold your nose and down 'er quick," the apron advised. "Go ahead, drink it."

"Drink it yourself," Stumpy said with considerable dignity. "Me, I've got some consideration for my stummick."

He stalked stiffly out of the saloon and wandered aimlessly along the planking. Confound it, life was a stacked deck with all the aces hid and the joker turning up no matter how a feller cut the cards! Everything in the world had happened to Stumpy lately, and none of it had been good.

There was the scanty consolation of reflecting that since the worst had happened to him, the worst was over, and it was while this thought was in his mind that he encountered little Launcelot Bartholomew.

"And how do you find the world using you this fine morning, Mr. Grampis?" Launcelot inquired politely.

Stumpy ran a bleak eye over the boy, from Lord Fauntleroy suit to yellow curls, and contemplated mayhem. Then a guileful look came over Stumpy's leathery face. Little Launcelot, a burr under a saddle blanket if ever a human was, had a certain ingenuity to him; and whereas that ingenuity had heretofore contributed not one whit to

Stumpy's happiness, Launcelot might be a formidable ally if he could be enlisted in a cause. Summoning a snaggle-toothed smile, Stumpy said, "You wouldn't have a notion how a man could lay his hands on a drink, now would you? Need it to ease the pain of an old bullet wound."

"You mean an intoxicating drink?" Launcelot inquired, his eyes big.

"Doctor's orders," Stumpy explained.

Launcelot pursed his lips thoughtfully. "There's none being sold in town, you know."

"I heard it hinted," said Stumpy.

"I'll tell you what," said little Launcelot. "The *pater* has some imported cigars which have been soaked in rum. Quite often, after he smokes one, he takes to singing. Do you suppose some of those cigars would ease your agony, Mr. Grampis?"

"It's worth a try," Stumpy decided and, for the first time to-day the sun shone for him.

"Come along," said Launcelot. "The *pater* doesn't approve of his cigars being given away, but it is obvious you are in misery. Those cigars cost a dollar each."

"Humph!" said Stumpy. "I usually get me forty cigars for that kind of money!"

Together they tip-toed into the Traveller's Rest and up the stairs. In the hallway, Launcelot raised a pink finger to his cherubic lips and motioned Stumpy to wait while Launcelot eased into the room he shared with his father. Shortly, he returned, closing the door quietly behind him, and under his arm was a cigar box. This he extended to Stumpy. "Help yourself, Mr. Grampis," Launcelot said.

Now here, Stumpy decided, was really something! He had never before smoked a drink, but there came that desperate hour when a man might be willing to combine all his vices. He snapped open the lid and instantly hurled the box away from him. "*Yeow!*" Stumpy shrieked, for a long green snake had jack-in-the-boxed out at him. Stumpy had wanted a snake and he'd found one. "Stomp on it!" he shouted wildly. "Stomp on the critter before it bites somebody!"

And then the eldritch laughter of little Launcelot was in his ears; and at the same time Stumpy saw that the snake was made out of cloth, stuffed, probably, with cotton, and dyed a hideous green. That cigar box was a trick affair, designed to launch a nightmare into the face of the unsuspecting person who opened it. Mad as a hornet with singed wings and a jumping toothache, Stumpy reached for little Launcelot, who raised a hurried call for help which fetched open the door Launcelot had just closed. Bartholomew B. Bartholomew stood there.

"Quiet!" B. B. whispered hoarsely. "Grampis, you're a little old to be playing childish games! Don't you two realise the doctor is operating in this very building?"

"He scared the liver out of me!" Stumpy protested, "He sprung a stuffed snake on me!"

B. B. looked sad and stricken. "He did? He sprung it on me the first day he got that contraption. I sympathise with you, Grampis. In fact——" Temptation tore at Bartholomew, twisting his face.

"Don't you do it, *pater*!" Launcelot protested. "Have you forgotten how I saved the day for you when you needed coolies so badly?"

"No, but I haven't forgotten either that it has taken us ever since to straighten out traffic after the way you tied it up by using the despatcher's key. Launcelot, sometimes you are very trying." He sighed. "If I let you spank him, Grampis, he'll probably send a letter to the Chicago office. He happens to rate high with them at the moment. He sent them a full report on how *he* saved the labour situation."

Stumpy gingerly picked up the stuffed snake. Perhaps he could persuade the bartender that he had indeed been bitten! But no, that snake would never stand the test of daylight. Muttering, Stumpy marched down the stairs and out of the hotel. There was nothing to do but board the work-train and wait for its departure to end-of-steel; and this he did, scrooching down into a seat and frowning blackly. It had been another difficult day.

"A cigar, Grampis?" someone said over Stumpy's shoulder, and Stumpy rose three feet off the seat. Behind him sat Abner Grubb, also headed for end-of-steel. The banker was extending his cigar case.

"*Gr-r-r-r!*" Stumpy growled.

Soon the train chugged out of Tailholt, and Stumpy looked with jaundiced eye upon the flat country that swept by. Confound it, it was little to ask of a cruel world, just a wee drop of a drink. He was a pore thirsty lamb with his tongue hanging out, and he could go baa-a-a-ing his heart away for all anybody cared. The train crossed the high, spider-legged trestle which spanned the only gorge between Tailholt and the canyon country, and Stumpy looked down into the bottomless depth and wondered how little Launcelot would like being dropped from here. A plague on bright children and Blue-Ribbon minded spinsters!

Over above the Weetigos clouds were gathering, and it looked like rain. A dinosaur had walked the last time it stormed; and Stumpy wondered, with a surge of interest, if the same thing might happen again. He craved to see one of those dinosaurs. And now he was remembering something Launcelot had said on Stumpy's first day in Tailholt: "Dinosaurs are any of certain extinct land reptiles," Launcelot had explained. Reptiles? Snakes were reptiles, too! Stumpy wondered if a man would qualify for a drink if he were bitten by a dinosaur. And how would one go about finding a dinosaur and getting himself bitten?

For a moment he was enraptured by the possibilities of the idea, and then he had a picture of himself wandering through a maze of canyons, a saucer of canned milk in his extended hand, crying, "Dinny? Here, Dinny? Where are you, Dinny?" and the whole project seemed utterly futile.

Stumpy, that thirsty lamb, settled down with a sigh. He'd have to keep right on being thirsty. But soon he'd be at end-of-steel, and there he would get the loan of a horse and take off to join Rowdy at the Sober Swede mine. Maybe, with luck, if that storm didn't shape up too fast and make travelling hard, he'd reach Humpback Hill by nightfall. . . .

17 : The Phantom Spur

In the shuddering darkness of the Sober Swede, Rowdy waited with Doctor Quong's voice echoing eerily, and Quong himself off there somewhere, invisible in the gloom but all too present, all too dangerous. It was a situation to raise the hackles on a man's neck. Rowdy had sampled the ruthlessness of this renegade Chinese who was anathema, even to his own people, and he had no doubt but that Quong would unhesitatingly shoot him down. The only question was why Quong hadn't already done so. Whatever secret this sealed mine possessed was not to be shared— Quong had made that mighty plain. The man didn't intend that Rowdy should leave alive.

"A condemned man is always allowed last words," Quong said sibilantly. "You wish to speak?"

There was more than magnanimity behind this offer, and suddenly Rowdy understood the intent of Quong's guile. The man had heard him come into the shaft, but Quong had lost whatever opportunity he'd had while Rowdy had been briefly silhouetted in the opening. So Quong was now running a sandy—Quong knew only that an intruder was in the mine, *but he didn't know Rowdy's exact whereabouts*! Hence Quong's challenge and invitation to speak. Here was Oriental cunning; Rowdy was to betray himself and then the bullet would come.

Easing his own gun out of its holster, Rowdy crouched down cautiously. Let Quong speak again, and the Chinese was going to learn that his little ruse could be a double-edged sword. But Quong was obviously wary; Quong must have guessed that Rowdy had seen through the game, for the man didn't again urge Rowdy to speak. Rowdy felt behind him; a wall of the shaft was to his back. He edged along this wall a foot or two, thankful that he'd discarded his boots, but feeling hemmed in, feeling buried alive. Sound rolled in these ghostly depths, and Rowdy almost came out of his skin. Then he realised that thunder had spoken over Humpback, and he remembered the overcast skies and his feeling that a storm was brewing.

He strained his ears, trying to catch the faintest footfall that might indicate that Quong, too, was manoeuvring. He heard nothing. The Chinese were a nocturnal people, but Quong apparently didn't have the eyes of a cat. Rowdy waited, his nerves twanging, his every faculty concentrated on the grim need of locating his enemy. And then, suddenly, sound was again in this shaft, a voice calling from the entrance: "Rowdy—? You in there, Rowdy, old hoss?"

And that was Stumpy Grampis!

At first it seemed so utterly incredible that Stumpy was here that it made Rowdy's head spin. Then he remembered that he'd commissioned Stumpy to follow him to this place, and there had indeed been time enough for Stumpy to overtake him. But now horror engulfed Rowdy, for Stumpy was coming into the mine, and if he raised his voice to warn Stumpy he would betray his own whereabouts to Quong; but if he kept silent, he would let Stumpy come to his doom. Quong would be able to line sights on Stumpy as the little man clogged the entrance.

Whereupon Rowdy in desperation felt along the floor until his fingers closed upon a small rock. He sent this rock whizzing across the shaft; it struck the far wall and caromed; and Quong fired, his gun flash lighting the gloom and revealing him against the opposite wall, his smile gone now and his lips drawn back from his teeth. Rowdy fired, too, his shot blending with Quong's and stirring up thunderous echoes, but Rowdy felt that he had missed, too. The cosmic thunder rolled again, as though the skies were trying to buy into this fight, and Rowdy chose that clamorous moment to slide along the wall a good six feet or more. In him was this much satisfaction: he had warned Stumpy.

He glanced towards the dim entrance, which was almost invisible now, with the night gathering swiftly outside. No sign of Stumpy. But the situation within the mine hadn't changed; Quong was still somewhere yonder, his gun ready, and the Chinese must be doubly desperate. Rowdy wondered if the ruse of a tossed rock might work again. He began groping for a rock, and then there was a frenzy of sound in the gloom, a whooshing of breath and many muttered curses and some sibilant squealing.

"I got him, Rowdy!" Stumpy shouted. "I got him!"

Stumpy had seized the opportunity to get inside the shaft while Rowdy had kept Quong busy for a moment! Fumbling his way from one wall to the other, Rowdy oriented himself by the sounds of the struggle; but Stumpy needed no help. "Got him pinned down and I'm sitting on his brisket," Stumpy announced triumphantly. "Spotted him in his gun flash. Light a match, Rowdy."

Rowdy scraped one aglow. Doctor Quong lay spread-eagled, his face a yellow mask of anger, his arms held down by Stumpy's knees. Stumpy had wrenched the man's gun away in the struggle; and Rowdy, spying the weapon on the rocky floor of the shaft, kicked it aside. "Tie him up, Stumpy," Rowdy ordered. "Use anything—his belt or your own. But search him good. He may have another gun."

Stumpy busied himself, while Rowdy lighted more matches. "No gun," Stumpy announced. "But here's candles in his inside coat-pocket."

Quong had come prepared to light his way after all. But Rowdy readily understood why Quong hadn't used his candles. The man had heard Rowdy on the rock-pile outside and had stayed in the dark to waylay the intruder. Rowdy lighted one of the candles, and in this illumination Stumpy finished trussing the Chinese, using the man's belt and Stumpy's own neckerchief. This done, the partners propped Quong against the wall in a sitting position. The man hissed like a wet cat and struggled wildly with his bonds.

Stumpy lighted another candle and held it high, sending shadows dancing eerily on the walls. Outside, the thunder still muttered, and Rowdy repressed a shudder. He wanted mightily to be out of this ancient mine; but he wanted, too, to see what it held.

Stumpy cried, "Look, Rowdy! A case of dynamite! And some caps and fuse."

Rowdy glanced at the indicated objects; they lay heaped against one wall, dust and cobwebs draping them. "Something left over from the days when this hole in the hill was being dug," Rowdy judged.

Doctor Quong said, "If you are wise, you will free me. Do so and I shall overlook this indignity."

Stumpy, who'd grown at least three feet in stature as a result of his accomplishment, said, "Shut up! You want me to gag you with one of your own shoes?"

Rowdy said with considerable feeling, "Quong, you're a disgrace to your people! I always respected Chinese till I met you. They've been among the best citizens of the West, hard-working, honest, and loyal. They're real pioneers. If it hadn't been for them, the railroads wouldn't have got built."

"No," said Stumpy with equal heat, "and the laundry wouldn't have got washed, either!"

Quong said, "I suggest you spare me the lecture." His eyes gleamed in the candlelight. His eyes were baleful.

"I'm just wasting my breath," Rowdy conceded. "But I had to get something off my chest." He glanced at Stumpy and raised an affectionate hand to his partner's shoulder. "You tied up a neat package, Stumpy."

"I shore did," Stumpy agreed. "Stopped off at Hatter's ranch on the way, and the crew told me where I'd find this here mine. I was plumb flabbergasted to see it open.

But I figgered maybe you'd clawed away those rocks, Rowdy, after fetching them tools from end-o'-steel."

Rowdy said, "Quong did the digging. Did you get Hatter to Tailholt without any sizable trouble?"

"Right, old hoss," said Stumpy. "And the doctor got there from Helena. He operated on Hatter this morning. I left before he was finished, but when I got to end-o'-steel, that big Scotsman with the whiskers had got a report over the telegraph wire. Hatter come through the operation fine as frawg's fur and was sleeping hisself a big sleep. He'll be fit as fiddle strings, Rowdy."

Rowdy said reflectively, "He should be safe enough in Tailholt."

"Taisy's gonna fetch him home to-night," Stumpy went on. "That come over the wire, too, because Champion wanted McAllister to keep the track clear for Bartholomew's special train to come back through. I gathered that the sawbones said it would be all right to move Hatter if they moved him gentle, and Taisy figgers she can take better care of him at the ranch than she can in the Traveller's Rest."

Quong began to laugh, a high, squeaking laugh that was not good to hear; and the echoes made it worse. Quong said, "You fools! You blind, deluded fools! Can you not recognise his danger? Release me, and I shall tell you how Hatter can be saved. Otherwise he is doomed. Are you too stupid to understand that?"

Rowdy contemplated him thoughtfully. "The only one who has been gunning for Hatter isn't apt to be gunning for him again, Quong. Just what are you driving at?"

"Free me and I shall talk."

"You'll talk," Rowdy announced grimly. "I'm going to see to that. I've collected a few pieces of a puzzle along the trail. I think you can fill in the gaps. But first I want to know what got you into such a sweat about this mine. Come on, Stumpy, let's have a look around."

Stumpy knelt and examined Quong's bonds, testing

them thoroughly, satisfying himself that they would hold. Overhead, the thunder boomed again, closer this time, it seemed; and again Rowdy felt the need to be out of this place. But, holding a candle above his head, he began groping deeper along the shaft, Stumpy at his elbow. And in this manner they came upon the skeleton.

It lay at the far end of the shaft; it lay there, a litter of bones with wisps of clothes clinging to it, the sightless sockets of the skull peering up at them, and Stumpy gasped. "Jumpin' Jehoshaphat!" he ejaculated. "A dead one!"

"A long time dead," Rowdy said softly.

"Hatter's crew told me this ole mine got sealed up by a rockslide," Stumpy said. "This pore devil must have been inside when it happened. That was mighty tough luck. Just think of him in here, gasping for air, dying slow."

Rowdy crouched down and held the candle closer. "He didn't die slow, Stumpy. Look at that skull! He was fetched a clout that did for him. Do you savvy, Stumpy? This man was murdered and left here, and when the mine got sealed it became his tomb."

"Pore devil," Stumpy said.

Rowdy began looking for something that would identify the skeleton—a belt buckle, a watch, anything that would have withstood the ravages of time. There was only a spur—a single spur on one of the boots. Very carefully Rowdy unfastened the spur and turned it over in his hands and then extended it to Stumpy.

"Take a look!" Rowdy said.

Stumpy frowned in puzzlement. "The jigger was only wearing one spur?"

Rowdy's voice betrayed his excitement. "I forgot. You never saw the spur that has been causing all the hullabaloo. This is the mate of it—this is the other spur. Stumpy, I kind of got thinking about the first spur as being a phantom spur, since it seemed to come and go like a ghost. But here's the real phantom—the missing spur. Do you see what it means?"

Stumpy was more puzzled than ever. "It don't help none. It doesn't have the name of this jigger scratched on it."

"Now I can guess who he was," said Rowdy. "Big Tom McMasters. The absconding banker whose dummy those boys were hanging the first night we came to Tailholt. Only he didn't abscond, Stumpy. Can't you savvy it? He was brought here and murdered and then this mine was sealed so he'd never be found."

"Jumpin' Jehoshaphat!" Stumpy ejaculated again. "I'm beginning to see a little light!"

Overhead the thunder tore the sky asunder, but even above that sound the laughter of Doctor Quong reached to the partners. "Now will you turn me loose, you stupid ones? Or will you stand there making senseless talk while Mad Hatter dies?"

But Rowdy had perked his ears to another sound, and his fingers closed on Stumpy's arm. "What was that?"

"Thunder," Stumpy decided.

"Fetch the candle," Rowdy urged his partner and went stumbling along the shaft, past the trussed Doctor Quong. At the entrance end, Rowdy came down upon his hands and knees, urging Stumpy to hold his candle closer.

"Blocked!" Rowdy cried. "Somebody rolled a boulder into the entrance just as the thunder sounded. Stumpy, get your shoulder against it. Now! Together! Heave!"

"It won't budge!" Stumpy moaned. "There must be other rocks backing it. Rowdy, we've been buried alive! There's gonna be *four* skeletons in this old mine! Doggone it, Rowdy, I'm getting too old for the kind of fool nonsense a feller runs into when he's taggin' around with you!"

When Rowdy Dow and Stumpy Grampis had come to the Weetigo country, they'd ridden into the heart of a mystery that had first manifested itself when Pocatello had stopped a stagecoach to try wresting a spur from Miss Arabella Hatter. Pocatello's play had seemed senseless to Rowdy, but Rowdy had bought cards, and in Tailholt later he'd faced a larger mystery. Someone had wanted—likewise against all reason—to keep Montana Central's tracks from pushing towards Porphyry, and it had been the partners' job to fight against the forces that harassed the steel. Thus Rowdy had come to learn that the two mysteries were somehow intertwined—the one that pertained to a spur a man might wear upon his boot, the other that involved a railroad spur.

He'd put a few pieces of a puzzle together in the ensuing days, and here in the depths of the Sober Swede he had stumbled upon a secret that completed the pattern. But he had found the remains of Big Tom McMasters only to find himself facing a fate comparable to that which had overtaken the cow-town banker; and in the first moment of realisation, a blind panic swept Rowdy that had him hurling his shoulder futilely against the rocks that clogged the mine entrance. Stumpy, too, was desperate, and they struggled until the sweat rolled from them. Then a measure of sanity came back to Rowdy, and he gave up the fruitless task.

"Stumpy," he demanded, "where was Abner Grubb the last time you saw him?"

"Why, he came out to end-o'-steel on the same work train as me," Stumpy replied, when he could catch his breath.

"He heard about Hatter coming through the operation okay? And how Taisy was figuring on bringing him home?"

Stumpy nodded. "He was there when McAllister got the word. I don't recollect that I saw him after that."

Rowdy turned back to where they'd left Doctor Quong. "You're laughing inside, you yellow devil!" Rowdy said. "Just as you laughed the other night when Grubb came to your camp. Can't you savvy that you're locked in here, too? When your big boss nailed a lid on our coffin, he likewise sealed yours."

Quong's shrug was wholly Oriental. "You had a chance to free me and you chose not to. Now it is too late."

"Damn it, man, I'm not thinking about us! Where and when will Grubb hit at Hatter? That's what I want to know!"

A flicker of expression crossed Quong's inscrutable face. "You have guessed?"

"The minute I realised it was Tom McMasters who was hidden in here. Who else stood to gain by murdering McMasters but his cashier? Grubb took over the bank and pocketed the funds that were supposed to have gone south with McMasters. It wouldn't do you a speck of good to cover up for Grubb, Quong. Yes, I can see that you've been playing his game and double-crossing him at the same time. He did the same to you. Last night, at Hatter's he shot Hatter through a bedroom window from the gallery, then shouted your name and made us believe you were the bushwhacker. We were fools enough to fall for it. But the point is that Grubb didn't kill Hatter, as he'd intended. Now I want to know where he'll make the try again."

Quong said thoughtfully, "So he fashioned a noose for my poor neck. . . ."

"You already had an air-dance coming to you. There

have been dead men in the construction camp. Grubb was just covering tracks for himself."

Quong's eyes gleamed. "You recall the trestle which spans a gulch between Tailholt and the canyon country?"

"I remember it."

"Many weeks ago, Grubb remarked that Montana Central's spur could be crippled seriously if anyone wrecked that trestle. He considered such an endeavour too risky, except in the case of a crisis. If I were Abner Grubb to-night, reflecting upon Mad Hatter being borne homeward after an operation that has perhaps lifted the veil of forgetfulness from Hatter's shadowed mind, I would be reflecting upon that trestle. I would be contemplating large truth: if train should be dropped into gorge, Hatter's lips would be forever sealed."

Rowdy groaned. "Everybody will be on that train—Bartholomew, his boy, Taisy, Champion." He was stricken with the thought that he had learned what he'd wanted to learn, but the knowledge had come too late. He knew now who'd rolled rocks to seal the entrance, long ago and again to-night. "I said I was going to the Sober Swede," he recalled. "I said it when Grubb was standing close by."

Stumpy suddenly leaped a foot into the air. "The dynamite, Rowdy! The *dynamite*!"

And then Rowdy remembered, too, remembered what he'd forgotten in the excitement of greater discoveries, remembered the cobweb shrouded case of dynamite that they'd found here. Big Tom McMasters hadn't been able to use that dynamite to free himself. Big Tom had been dead when he'd been left here. But Rowdy had hands and the strength to use them, and he went plunging towards that rotted wooden case and clawed into it. He got a stick of dynamite and a short fuse and used his teeth to crimp a cap.

"Come along, Stumpy!" he cried. "I've never heard tell of dynamite getting so old it got useless!"

Again they went clambering towards the clogged entrance, and here they worked to wedge the stick of dynamite beneath the boulder, and when this was done they touched the stub of candle to the fuse. They scurried along back the shaft, pausing to seize Doctor Quong and lift him bodily and bear him to the far end where Tom McMasters' skeleton lay sprawled. Rowdy said, in a voice that sounded strangely alien in his ears, "We've got to hope that it doesn't bring down the roof of this shaft."

Stumpy squeezed himself hard against the wall and put his hands over his hairy ears. "Wish this Chinese galoot was bigger. We ought to use him for a barricade."

"I——" said Rowdy, but the dynamite went *Harumpf*! and a mighty backwash of wind smote the partners hard, pressing them against the rock and extinguishing the candles, and an acrid smell was in the air; stifling dust rose, and it was raining rocks. For a moment they were half-stunned by the force of the concussion, and then they were groping back down the shaft, groping towards the entrance, and Stumpy let out a wild, *"Yipp-ee-ee!"* He pounded Rowdy's back. "She's open, old hoss! She's open!"

"Pile out," said Rowdy. "The gent who rolled the rocks isn't waiting with a gun. He's heading hell-bent for that trestle."

They wormed their way outside, dragging Quong after them, and they found rain in the air and the thunder muttering overhead and the dark night all around. Rowdy went clambering over the rubble and at a certain point fell upon his hands and knees and began groping. "Left my boots hereabouts," he explained. "Maybe that explosion buried them."

"Here's one," Stumpy said.

"And here's the other. Just a minute till I stomp into them."

Stumpy said, "I left my horse back a piece. I hope that big noise didn't send it bolting."

Rowdy was hoping the same thing as regarded his own

mount, but he found the horse still tied behind the ancient shack. Stumpy's had been firmly fastened to a small tree. Rowdy turned to their silent captive. "You must have a mount nearby. Where is it?"

Quong shook his head. "I would be most foolish to assist you in taking me to my doom."

Rowdy grasped him roughly. "I've got no time to waste on you! Not with the ride we've got to make tonight. You'll lead us to your horse, or you'll go back into the mine and we'll block the entrance. And you'll wait there tied up, savvy, till such time as we get back to let you out."

Quong was thoughtful. "You are a foolhardy man who might well die before this night is over. I prefer prison with *live* keeper. My horse is in the brush over there on the other side of the rockslide."

"That's better," said Rowdy.

They found Quong's horse and hoisted him to the saddle; and Rowdy, aboard his own horse, took the reins of Quong's mount. "Let's ride, Stumpy," he said, and they were off, heading due east towards Hatter's ranch.

It was a ride to remember for many days to come—in fact, it was a ride to bring a man sitting upright in his blankets and sweating on future nights, for it was made of the stuff of nightmares. The darkness pressed down hard, and the rain pelted, and the sky growled overhead, only intermittent lightning flashes illuminating the way. They had to ride by instinct, trusting to the horses to find sure footing, and more than once Rowdy was certain he would be catapulted from his saddle. He spared neither himself nor the mount, and was oblivious to the shrill squawks of terror which came often from Quong. Rowdy had an objective, and his job was to reach it and his prayer was that he wouldn't be too late. The lights of Hatter's ranch, flickering dimly across the openness, were his beacon, and finally they came thundering into the ranch-yard, their horses heaving.

Their wild entry brought Hatter's crew spilling from

the bunkhouse, but upon them Rowdy wasted little time in explaining. "Take this slant-eyed son and keep him tied," he ordered. "In fact, you'd better take turns sitting on his chest until somebody shows up to collect him. He's bad medicine, and he's slippery. Now rope out a couple of fresh horses for me and my pard. Don't ask questions. We're doing this for your boss."

While the change was being made, Rowdy turned to Hatter's foreman. "You been with Hatter a long time?" Rowdy asked.

"Nearly twenty years."

"You recollect when it was Hatter got that scar on his head?"

"Lemme see . . . Better than ten years ago. Someone took a pot-shot at him from the brush. Never did know who. I remember now—it was the year after the bank went bust. We got thinking that a heap of bad luck was shore coming all at once."

As the partners swung up into leather again, Rowdy said, "Abner Grubb ridden through here to-night?"

"He stopped a short while ago and borrowed a horse," Hatter's foreman explained. "Said he was doing some riding for the railroad. Fetched us news that Hatter might be home to-night. He seemed mighty glad."

"I'll bet," Rowdy said dryly.

"You gonna collect Quong later?" Stumpy asked. "What you aim to do with him? Turn him over to some sheriff?"

"I'll hand him over to Hop Gow," Rowdy said. "It was Hop's tong he double-crossed in 'Frisco, wasn't it? Montana Central owes old Hop something. We'll let the Chinese take care of their own."

Then they were riding again, and if the first stage of this journey had been a nightmare, the next miles were the sort of nightmare that a nightmare had. For they were into the canyons soon, and the rain beat down harder, and now they were men moving in a blind pocket of darkness. But

Rowdy had remembered the road Taisy had taken and he sought out this road and followed it. Sometimes that lightning came, and he was glad of that, for in the darkness he was sometimes sure he was hopelessly lost and travelling in circles. This storm rivalled the one of a few nights back, and Rowdy remembered that the dinosaurs walked on such nights, but he would have taken on a dinosaur single-handed to-night and kicked it out of his path. He was that desperate.

"Where's that dog-gone construction camp?" Stumpy wailed in the darkness. "We musta missed it a mile."

"Stop!" a voice roared up ahead. "Faith, and it's a bullet ye'll be gettin' in your bellies!"

The lightning flashed, and they saw one of the graders blocking the trail, a rifle held ready; but Rowdy sang out, naming himself and his partner. The grader came forward till he stood at Rowdy's stirrup. "Pass on," the man said. " 'Tis a watch we're keeping to-night, me bhoys. When the thunder rolls is when thim big b'asts walk."

Rowdy said, "McAllister here?"

"A-mutterin' in thim whiskers of his."

"Good!" cried Rowdy and urged his horse onward.

Around a turn of the canyon they came upon the camp; fires burned ahead, and men milled about, and big among them was Avalanche McAllister. To the Scot Rowdy went at once, dropping down from his saddle. "Grubb been here?" Rowdy barked.

"The banker mon? He rode in just a wee bit ago. Seems I seen him putterin' around. He's nae here now."

Rowdy groaned. "Grubb was stealing explosives!" he judged. "And no one would have paid him heed; the graders would practically figure him to be a railroad official. Tell me, McAllister: has Bartholomew's train left Tailholt?"

The big Scot nodded. "Hoots, mon, and ye're in something of a lather! 'Tis true the train is on its way. None other than the vice-president himself wired me to have the tracks cleared. 'Tis waiting for the gr-rand arrival we are."

Rowdy said frantically, "Get one of your locomotives headed towards Tailholt—and mighty fast! We'll be riding in it, Stumpy and me. Don't stand there gaping! The trestle's going to be blasted to-night! And Bartholomew's train will be dumped in the gorge while we're growing roots!"

He gave McAllister a push and that broke the trance that held the giant Scot. The man went charging towards a siding where a locomotive stood; then he was lost in the sheeting rain. Rowdy dragged at Stumpy and went running after McAllister. The partners clambered into the cab. McAllister was already there. "You're sure, mon," he asked, "that you know what you're talking about? 'Twill be a dangerous run!"

Rowdy said, "Don't argue! Get this thing rolling."

"I can fasten on a flat car, ye ken, and tak' half my crew along."

"One man can do the job that needs to be done. Keep your boys here. There's Pocatello to think about. His outfit might hit the camp while we're gone."

Stumpy said, "Where's a shovel? I'll get this contraption a-goin'!"

The fireman stared at the leathery little man. "*You,* again!" he ejaculated, for this was the same crew and the same locomotive that had carried Stumpy on his historic run to Helena.

"Don't give me no talk," Stumpy said with a frown. "Danger's ahead. You want to be a hero, don't you?"

"If it pays time and a half," said the fireman.

The drivers spun and caught, steam hissed, and the locomotive moved eastward, the headlamp forcing a tunnel of light through the rain-filled darkness. With the whistle screaming, the engine chugged out of the canyons, the five in the cab silent, those not otherwise occupied leaning out to scan the track ahead. A mile fell behind and another; and Rowdy measured time and distance, remembering that

Grubb must be travelling by horseback. Had the man got a fresh horse at the construction camp? Rowdy had not thought to ask.

"I hope ye aren't making a mistake, lad," Avalanche McAllister said with a shake of his head.

And now Rowdy understood the nature of McAllister's fear, for there was no way of signalling the train up ahead, the train that was bearing westward out of Tailholt; for semaphores hadn't yet been set up on this raw new spur. And so they could only barge blindly through the sheeting rain, plunging onward along a track with another train bearing down upon them from the opposite direction. Even discounting Abner Grubb and the last desperate play which Rowdy was sure the man was attempting to-night, the makings of calamity lay in this wild ride.

This was no way to run a railroad!

19 : Rowdy Speaks

Avalanche McAllister spoke not many minutes later, pressing his lips close to Rowdy's ear. " 'Tis a'most to the trestle we are, mon."

Rowdy leaned from the cab for a look. "Stop this contraption," Rowdy ordered. "Better douse the light or we'll be Grubb's targets."

McAllister spoke to the engineer; the locomotive screeched to a stop; and Rowdy was at once piling from the cab, Stumpy after him. Rowdy got the impression that McAllister, too, came down to the ground; and perhaps the engineer and fireman followed, but he wasn't sure, and he didn't wait to discover if he were thus reinforced. Stumbling along the grade until he was clear of the locomotive, Rowdy got up between the rails and hurried forward, glad to have the ties to guide him. Lightning came, and he welcomed it; in the glare he saw the trestle ahead; and he saw, too, the scurrying figure of a man—a man who had darted off the trestle at this, its west end, and was now heading away from the tracks.

"Grubb!" Rowdy panted.

And Abner Grubb had spied them, too, for a gun-flash cut the darkness that came tromping on the heels of the lightning, the thunder of the gun lost in the thunder of the sky. Once, twice, Grubb fired, and the banker was still running as he fired, cutting overland and putting distance between himself and the trestle.

Stumpy cried, "We can head him off!"

"Let him go," Rowdy decided, dread choking him.

Grubb had undoubtedly got explosives from the construction camp. And Grubb had ridden hard to this trestle. Quong had surmised exactly what his master would do! But Grubb wouldn't have wanted to blast the trestle until the special train, roaring out of Tailholt, was almost upon the doomed structure. There was always the chance that if the trestle were destroyed in advance, someone might stumble upon the damage and flag the oncoming train. Therefore Grubb would have waited till the train was near, then fired a fuse and taken off. So Rowdy reasoned. And far down the track to the east Rowdy saw the light of Bartholomew's train. This wasn't the time to be squandering precious seconds pursuing Grubb!

No, let Grubb get his horse and take off! And Grubb's horse must be somewhere at this west end of the trestle. Now Rowdy was out upon the spidery structure, Stumpy wheezing along behind him; and Rowdy plunged forward in the darkness, mindful that if he tripped he might fall off the trestle. The lightning came again, and Rowdy spied what he sought—a bundle of dynamite sticks lashed to one of the rails in the very centre of the structure, a sputtering fuse trailing from the bundle—all too short a fuse! This glimpse Rowdy got, and butterflies stampeded through his stomach. Then, in the descending darkness, Rowdy sprinted forward and dived, falling upon the red eye of the fuse and tugging frantically. The rail, so close to his ear, throbbed to the oncoming train.

"Get up ahead and flag that train, Stumpy!" Rowdy roared as the fuse came free in his hand.

Stumpy dashed on past him, stumbling and lurching, while Rowdy tugged at the twine with which Grubb had lashed the dynamite. He got the deadly package freed and hurled it far out into the gorge, then pulled himself slowly to his feet. Up ahead Stumpy stood silhouetted in the growing light of the oncoming engine, the little man standing in the middle of the track waving his arms frantically. Stumpy might yet have to leap aside and let the train careen onwards to smash into the darkened locomotive on the west side of the trestle! But Bartholomew's train was grinding to a stop, and Rowdy was suddenly so weak with relief that he needed something to lean against.

There was no visible support except Avalanche McAllister, who had come venturing out upon the trestle. The big Scot looming in the darkness, Rowdy said, "You can back that cast-iron cayuse of yours to the construction camp. We saved the day—or the night, rather. And it's the sloppiest night I ever saved."

McAllister sighed. " 'Tis grey I'm growin', wor-rkin' for the r-railroad!"

Rowdy glanced to the west. No sense taking off after Abner Grubb. The man would be up into the saddle and keeping himself far from the track. Rowdy lurched on across the trestle and came into the blinding glare of the headlamp of Bartholomew's stopped train. Here he found Stumpy surrounded by a knot of excited, questioning people, including Champion, Bartholomew, Taisy, and little Launcelot. Stumpy was playing the rôle of The Man Who Flagged The Train with considerable gusto. Rowdy said, "Let's get out of the rain and get moving. We can do the talking aboard. Me, I'll breathe easier when your cargo is safe at end-of-steel. By the way, how is Hatter?"

"Doing fine," Champion replied. "He came through the operation splendidly. A rugged constitution there. He's been sleeping ever since."

Rowdy clambered up the steps of Bartholomew's private car and let himself into the lighted elegance of its interior, doffing his sombrero and spilling rain from its brim on to the luxurious carpeting. The others clambered aboard after him; the drivers spun and caught, and the train moved onwards. Rowdy let himself into a plush chair, thrust out his legs and smiled.

"What is all this?" B. B. demanded. "Grampis said something about an attempt to dynamite the trestle. Claimed Grubb was behind it. That's incredible!"

Rowdy said, "So? Shall I spin you a bedtime story?"

"We're all mighty curious," Bartholomew conceded.

Rowdy closed his eyes. "To savvy everything, you've got to go back thirteen years, to a time when the Tailholt bank was run by a man named Tom McMasters, who had a cashier named Abner Grubb. Grubb schemed a scheme to make himself rich. He talked his boss into taking a ride to Humpback Hill. How he did that I don't know, but it must have been easy enough. They were supposed to be friends. Maybe he told McMasters that the Sober Swede was worth developing even though it had been given up by every prospector who'd peeked into it. Anyway, he either got McMasters into the mine or close to it. And he killed him by clouting him over the head."

Taisy drew in a long hard breath that was almost a sob, and Rowdy opened his eyes and glanced at her. "Yes, my dear," he said. "You can marry your man. You're not the daughter of a thief after all. It was Grubb who had the sticky fingers. He killed your dad and left him inside the Sober Swede and set off a rock-slide to seal the shaft. Grubb wouldn't have found that hard—he proved to-night that he's handy with explosives. Afterwards, he stripped the bank. All the signs said that McMasters had walked off with the money. Overnight Grubb had made himself rich, and he took over the ruined bank, built it up and made himself richer. Do you see how simple it was?"

Champion moved close to Taisy and put his arm around her, steadying her.

"But what has this got to do with the railroad?" Champion demanded. "Grubb was a friend of Montana Central; the railroad meant prosperity for this range and prosperity for him. Why should he have been trying to wreck us to-night?"

"He's been trying to wreck you all along—with the help of Doctor Quong and a gang of hardcase riders. You see, Grubb had pulled the perfect crime, except for one slight flaw. Before he sealed the Sober Swede, he stripped

McMasters of any kind of identification, just to make doubly sure that if the body were ever found it wouldn't be recognised. But he overlooked something—McMasters' spur. There was only one. McMasters must have lost the other that very night he'd ridden to his death, for *that* spur was found by a man who happened to be riding in that section, probably for the simple reason that he lived thereabouts—Mad Hatter."

Champion's eyes widened. "And Hatter recognised that the spur was McMasters'?"

Rowdy shook his head. "The way I figure it, he didn't. But he had it in his house; and Grubb, who visited there, must have seen it. So Grubb started worrying. How close had Hatter been the night Grubb had beefed McMasters? Would Hatter some day remember whose spur he'd found? If that happened, would he also remember the night he'd found it? Would things that hadn't meant anything to Hatter at the time start making sense? All those questions must have eaten at Grubb until he decided that the only way to keep the first murder secret was to do another. He took a shot at Hatter. I asked Hatter's foreman about his boss's old wound to-night, and I found out that Hatter got ambushed not long after McMasters disappeared. Grubb didn't kill Hatter, but the bullet robbed Hatter of his memory, and Grubb felt safe again."

Bartholomew frowned. "But didn't the spur go east to Miss Arabella Hatter?"

"Right as rain," Rowdy conceded. "Grubb would have probably stolen the spur from Hatter's ranch, if it hadn't. Miss Arabella wanted some trinket from the West, and Hatter sent her the spur. When Grubb found that out, he probably felt even safer. Hatter was no danger to him—not when Hatter couldn't remember the time of day. And the spur, which would have matched Tom McMasters' other spur if the mine ever got opened, was gone out of the country. Grubb could sit back and make his stolen dollars work for him."

"Now I'm beginning to see it," Champion said slowly. "We came along, all these years later, and proposed to drive a tunnel through Humpback. . . ."

Rowdy nodded. "Exactly. The mills of the gods that the poet fellow talked about had finally started grinding against Grubb. He'd covered his tracks and the years had gone by; and then, all of a sudden, here was a railroad with a notion of digging into Tom McMasters' grave! It must have given Grubb some mighty bad nights! Suppose McMasters' body was found. Any idiot could guess who'd beefed him, for only one man had gained. To make matters worse, there was a way McMasters could be identified, as long as that other spur was lying around loose somewhere. Grubb sweated, I'll bet you! He had to keep Montana Central from building towards Humpback at any cost. But he had to play his cards close to his vest and pretend to be a friend of the railroad. So he needed a partner."

Champion said, "I remember his saying at Hatter's ranch yesterday that he'd known Quong away back."

Again Rowdy nodded. "Grubb must have taken a couple of steps. First he got hold of Quong, and had Quong hire a bunch of hardcases to make things so rough for the railroad that you'd give up the spur you were building. And again Grubb got to thinking about that other spur, the one back East, the one that could put a rope around his neck if it got matched with the spur your tunnel-diggers might uncover. So Grubb wrote to Miss Arabella, pretending to be Mad Hatter, and urged her to come West and bring the spur. The day we rode the stagecoach with Miss Arabella, she mentioned that Hatter's handwriting looked feeble. She hadn't seen the real thing for years, so she didn't suspect the forgery. Grubb had a habit of fetching mail from town to Hatter's place, and my guess is that he steamed open Miss Arabella's letters from there on out. That way he knew when she'd be arriving. And he had his pard, Doctor Quong, ready and waiting to snatch the spur."

Stumpy said, "By grab, you was right about Quong signalling them boys to stop the stage!"

"Right as rain," said Rowdy. "But Quong was fixing to double-cross Grubb. Grubb probably had to trust Quong with the whole truth to persuade Quong to front for him in the fight against the railroad. Once Quong got the spur, he decided to make Grubb pay through his long nose. I've a hunch that shot Quong fired through the window in Tailholt was to give Grubb a hint that Quong was playing cards of his own. Grubb wouldn't have been expecting Quong to shoot at railroad people when *he* was in the crowd! In any case, Grubb lit out for Quong's camp, and I was there when he tried dickering with Quong. The Chink played cat-and-mouse, reminding Grubb that although Grubb was the real king wolf of the railroad raiders, those bodies didn't know it, so Grubb was in a split stick. Quong was thinking of having his boys open the Sober Swede. If he'd got McMasters' body and the *other* spur, too, he'd really have had Grubb over a barrel. He could have blackmailed him out of his back teeth."

"But you got the spur away from Quong," Champion pointed out.

"And turned it over to Hatter. Grubb had lit out for Hatter's, figuring the spur would be fetched there. Grubb had a bad day yesterday, while Hatter puzzled over that spur. Grubb was shaking in his boots for fear Hatter might remember things, seeing that spur again. Finally Grubb shot Hatter through the window, not in an attempt to get the spur but with the idea of shutting Hatter's mouth for good. He made us think Quong did that job, and all the sign being what it was, we were willing to bite. Grubb was alone with Hatter for a short time after that, while we were bringing the wagon round; but he didn't dare make another play against Hatter just then. He couldn't have pinned *that* on Quong—not with the crew out hunting Quong."

Champion said, "Grubb came to Tailholt when we

fetched Hatter on to town. He must have stuck with Hatter right through, hoping he'd get a real chance to finish the job he'd only half done at the ranch. And he must have started sweating again when the doctor proposed to cure Hatter's old wound."

"Grubb had two things to sweat about," Rowdy observed. "Hatter had mentioned the Sober Swede, which meant that Hatter had remembered that he'd first found the spur close to the old mine. And I'd said I was going to prowl that rockpile, and Grubb heard me. I found Quong opening the mine but Grubb came hurrying back from Tailholt and locked me and Stumpy and Quong inside. Then he lit out to take care of Hatter by blasting the trestle. He couldn't risk Hatter's having his memory restored. Grubb was mighty desperate then."

B. B. shook his head. "It still seems incredible. A man putting such resources against the railroad, just to keep us from driving a tunnel."

"The two things that meant the most to Grubb were at stake," Rowdy pointed out. "His money—and his neck. He'd have moved a mountain to have kept his killing of McMasters from coming to light. But he got so jittery he began making mistakes. His bad one was in trusting Quong. And he should have left the other spur back East instead of scheming to get Miss Arabella out here with it. Why, he even wanted to marry Taisy, and he's more than twice her age! You see, Taisy thought her father was a thief and she never forgave him for smearing the family name. Some day she intended running him down. That worried Grubb, too. If he could have married Taisy, he could have forbid her." Rowdy glanced at the girl. "His story about having heard from your dad in Central America was a cover-up, of course."

Taisy said, "The skunk!"

B. B. looked like a man who'd taken a fast ride on a merry-go-round. "Of course it was Grubb who sent McAllister that telegram discrediting you, Dow. I can see now that Grubb certainly didn't want a trouble-shooter on the job. But how did you deduce all this, Dow?"

"I got a piece of the puzzle here, a piece there. None of them seemed to fit. Not till I crawled into that old mine to-night and found a skeleton there. What made that skeleton as valuable as a gold vein? The fact that it wore a spur like one Grubb was willing to pay fifty thousand dollars for? Things began falling into place, then. I'd finally got the pattern."

Little Launcelot said, "Do you know, I don't believe I could have done a better job myself."

"I don't think you could have either," said Rowdy.

"Ha! Ha! Ha!" said Stumpy Grampis.

Bartholomew glanced apprehensively through one of the windows; rain laid silvery splinters upon the glass. "And Grubb? Where is he now?"

Rowdy's lips tightened. "Out yonder somewhere, still thinking of the same two things—his money and his neck. He'll think of doubling back to Tailholt, stuffing a suitcase, and clearing out. But as soon as we get to end-of-steel, we'll wire back and have Tailholt law looking for him. Grubb will expect us to do that, so maybe he's already forgotten about the money and will be thinking only of his neck. My guess is that he'll be heading into the canyons to look for Pocatello and the other railroad raiders. Quong probably told him where their camp is, since the two were in cahoots up till the double-cross. Now that the game is up, Grubb needn't keep silent. He can convince Pocatello that he was the paymaster, not Quong. He'll want those guns protecting him."

B. B. said, "Do you think the whole bunch will quit the country now?"

Rowdy shrugged. "I don't aim to give them the chance. When we get to end-of-steel, I want every worker to head into the canyons. We'll stomp that nest of snakes. The time has come to wind up the chores."

Champion frowned. "On nights like these the dinosaurs walk. We don't want to lose our new crew."

"Me," said Rowdy, "I pine to see a dinosaur again. I think I've got that figured out, too. In some respects Grubb picked the right man when he picked Quong. I've heard tell that the Chinese are the greatest illusionists on the face of the earth."

They hurtled towards end-of-steel without mishap, though after hearing Rowdy's recital a strange intentness held most of the passengers of Bartholomew's private car. Now they knew the whys and wherefores of the fight that had been made against Montana Central; but Abner Grubb, unmasked, was still on the loose and the fight was not yet finished.

Bartholomew B. Bartholomew took to pacing, jumpy as a barefooted man in a cactus patch. Mark Champion shared his superior's agitation; but Champion was devoting himself to Taisy, the two frequently vanishing into a partitioned-off end of the car where Mad Hatter slept. Even little Launcelot seemed preoccupied. From the frown on his face, it was obvious that Launcelot was considering some weighty problem. Stumpy, tired but very much satisfied with himself after having at last got in on the fun, found the darkest corner of the commodious car and sprawled out in a chair to snooze. Rowdy looked around.

"Where's Miss Arabella?" he asked, noticing now that she was not present.

B. B. looked pained. "She stayed in Tailholt. She wanted to investigate a rumour that one of the saloons was serving rootless root beer."

Soon the train came chugging into the construction camp; and Rowdy, peering from the window, saw that vast sea of tents in the light of huge fires which had been kept roaring through the rain, the workers feeding empty packing cases and barrels to the flames. Avalanche McAllister had got his engine backed into the camp; Rowdy glimpsed the big Scot among the milling men. Those in Bartholomew's car began dismounting, Stumpy rousing himself and coming to his feet, whereupon the little man tripped and plunged headlong across the carpeting.

"Confound it!" Stumpy roared. "Who tied my spurs together whilst I was snoozing?"

But little Launcelot was already out of the coach and gone into the night.

"I'm sorry, Grampis," B. B. said, helping Stumpy to his feet. "The boy once did that same thing to the shoelaces of the president of Montana Central when he came to dinner at our Chicago home. It cost me a promotion I'd been waiting years to get."

Stumpy fumbled with the piece of rawhide which had secured his spurs. "The day I quit working for the railroad, you'd better have that sprout back in Chicago!" he threatened wildly. "I'm going to bust him into small pieces."

"Work to do, Stumpy," Rowdy reminded him and left the coach.

With B. B. beside him, Rowdy went first to the telegrapher's shack; and the wires were made to hum as word went winging back to Tailholt to warn the town to be on the look-out for Grubb. Rowdy drew a sigh of relief upon learning that the wires were still up. Grubb hadn't found the means to cut them.

Hatter was left aboard the car, but Champion came into the telegrapher's shack before Rowdy and Bartholomew were finished. "Hatter's awake," Champion reported. "I talked to him a little, but I didn't want to tire him. He's verified much of your story about Grubb, Dow. Hatter never knew who shot him years ago, but he remembers now that that spur once belonged to Big Tom McMasters."

Champion glanced at B. B. "You'll be pleased to know, chief, that Hatter has had a change of heart as regards the railroad. Taisy told him how you rushed him to

Tailholt and brought a doctor in for him. I've got Hatter's word that we can have right of way across his ranch."

B. B. swelled visibly and cleared his throat. "The man's change of heart was inevitable," B. B. said. "Progress knows no insurmountable barrier. As one who has played no small part in forging the vast network of transportation which has pushed back the frontier, I feel free to say——"

"Say it to-morrow," Rowdy interjected. "This is no time for speech-making. I want an order passed to all the men who can be spared without leaving the camp unguarded. I want them into the canyons."

B. B. looked doubtful. "If the dinosaur walks, we'll have no Chinese in the crew by sun-up."

"I'm *hoping* a dinosaur walks," Rowdy said. "It's the only way we'll ever corral one. Get those boys to moving, B. B."

Bartholomew went away shaking his head, but shortly there was pandemonium in the camp. The voices of B. B. and Avalanche McAllister were bellowing orders; and men arming themselves with pick-handles and anything that might qualify as a club, began massing to march. Rowdy, after scanning a last wire from Tailholt which said that a search had been made there for Grubb and had failed, came out into the rain again. Stumpy had procured horses for the two of them and also rustled up a pair of tattered slickers, and Rowdy mounted and moved up to the head of the massed men.

"Sic 'em, boys," he said and pointed along the canyon. And so a motley army moved into the sleazy darkness, leaving the camp behind and trudging back over the rocky floor to where the canyon led into the one Rowdy was seeking. They came with considerable clamour; and Rowdy and Stumpy moved on up ahead of them, Rowdy pausing as they reached the mouth of each flanking canyon to send a handful of workers into it. The rain was as steady as ever, having neither slackened nor increased in intensity; the thunder still muttered, and there were occasional lightning flashes.

Champion, also mounted, came galloping up along the straggly line of Irish and Chinese, another rider with him. Champion said, "Dow? We'll never find anybody in these canyons!"

"The raiders will show themselves," Rowdy said. "I've been wondering all day where they were. Quong was figuring on having them help open the mine, but he did that job alone. He must have sent Pocatello's crew back into the canyons because a storm was shaping up. Pocatello would have expected such an order, seeing a new batch of Chinks was ripe to be stampeded. And now he'll figure there's only one way to take us off his tail."

Champion's voice held a puzzled note. "Are you trying to say that those railroad raiders have the power to make a dinosaur appear?"

"What better way to turn the Chinks back? Remember the other night," Rowdy peered hard. "That Taisy with you?"

The girl's bull whip cracked in the darkness. "It's me," she said.

Now they were far from camp, deep into the canyon Rowdy had prowled the night before looking for dragon tracks. It was hereabouts he had found them. The Chinese straggled behind him, their voices raised in some tuneless song; and Rowdy, to add to the bedlam, drew his gun and fired at the sky. Stumpy let out a wild *"Yipp-ee-ee!"* and slapped his sombrero against his thigh. "This dinosaur hunting is shore fun, Rowdy," Stumpy opined.

And then suddenly, there was one of those startling sequences of events such as Rowdy had experienced a few nights ago when he had first ridden this canyon in a rainstorm. The lightning came, revealing the pelting rain and the canyon walls looming on either side, and the boulder-littered floor. There was noise and confusion and all the world bathed briefly in a chalky glow. And there was that huge ghostly thing moving just ahead, moving in the downpour, something out of another age, something out of a nightmare.

Just for an instant it was revealed, and then the darkness blotted it out; and the voices of the Chinese rose, shrill with terror. But Rowdy was bawling to them to stand their ground; and at the same time Rowdy was urging his horse, not in the direction where that huge monster had loomed, but in the *opposite* direction, toward the other canyon wall. He almost caromed into that wall, and then he spilled from the saddle and began groping along the wall, seeking a ledge that tilted upward. There had to be such a ledge! The lightning came again, and he saw it. "They're up here," he called above the clamour. "Come and get 'em!"

Champion and Stumpy and Taisy were doing a good job of keeping the Chinese from stampeding, and the Irish had already recognised Rowdy's call to battle. Men were spilling down the ledge from some high shelf above—Pocatello and his crew—and guns began barking. But the Irish were upon the raiders, pick-handles swinging; and it was a fight of the likes to gladden the heart of Erin.

Through this mêlée Rowdy fought his way, toiling up that tilting ledge and having often to wield gun-barrel and fist. But Pocatello's crew, choking the trail at first, were outnumbered, and the ranks of the raiders thinned as Rowdy struggled upward. This ledge climbed the canyon wall like a gigantic ramp, levelling off about half-way up to become a wide shelf that ran endlessly above the canyon; and here Rowdy found a lone figure—a figure which greeted him with gun-fire. Abner Grubb fired once, then turned to bolt, running along the shelf; and Rowdy panted after him. But someone brushed by Rowdy, a bull whip cracking in the darkness. The long lash streaked out to wrap itself around Grubb's ankles. The man went down, and Rowdy fell upon him, but there was no fight in Grubb.

"Knocked out," Rowdy told Taisy.

"Dow, Taisy!" That was Mark Champion calling. He came groping along the shelf, and Rowdy asked, "How are things below?"

"Just about over. Those that didn't get away in the dark have either been laid out or captured by our boys. Was Grubb here?"

"Got him. He'd joined up with Pocatello, just as I'd thought."

As he spoke, Rowdy was fumbling along the rim, and shortly he found what he sought. The lightning flared to help him, and he pointed to what appeared to be a blanket tossed over a box. He jerked this blanket away and said, "Look!" But the darkness came again and none of them had more than a glimpse.

"What is it?" Champion demanded.

Rowdy was feeling the object with his hand. "What I finally guessed," he said. "A little old lime-lighted magic lantern using glass slides. Do you see how it was done, Champion? Quong found this shelf on the canyon wall, and it suited his purpose. Any time a raid was made, the Chinks were sure to come pouring into the canyons, fighting mad. Pocatello led them this way. His boys probably hid their horses up a piece, then climbed to this ledge. They had this magic lantern all set up to project against the opposite canyon wall, which makes a good screen. They waited till the Chinks were close by, and they also waited for a lightning flash. When the lightning came, they jerked away the blanket and flashed a glass slide picturing a dinosaur. They couldn't flash it in deep dark; somebody would have figured out that a real dinosaur couldn't be seen unless there was light. But even with the lightning, they were able to project, and the picture showing dim and ghostly."

"But glass slides are still pictures. The creature moved, Dow! I'll swear it did!"

"By jiggling the lantern a little, even a still picture could be made to look as if it was moving. Grubb must have removed the slide after that last projection, or I'd show you. This scheme was Quong's, I reckon; you'll remember that I said the Chinese were the world's greatest illusionists. He didn't miss a bet to give himself the best advantage—stormy nights, thunder and lightning, wild excitement in the air. It's a wonder those workers weren't seeing whole herds of dinosaurs!"

"But you said you found tracks, Dow!"

"That was the prize touch to make the illusion perfect. Look around, Mark. I'll bet we'll find some sort of gadget, made of wood likely, that would leave a dinosaur track if it was lowered from the canyon rim by a rope. With such a gadget they could make tracks practically anywhere, with no human tracks showing nearby. Quong was a palaeontologist. He'd know what a dinosaur track should look like."

"Here's the thing over here," Taisy called. "Feels like a hat-rack with a big base. And there's a length of rope fastened to it."

Champion said, "How did you guess all this, Dow?"

"I saw the dinosaur, remember. I couldn't get it out of my head. But it just wasn't a real dinosaur. I remembered that little Launcelot said they'd been extinct for a heap of years. There had to be a trick to it. All things considered, how else could that trick have been worked except with a magic lantern and a gadget for making tracks?"

Champion chuckled ruefully. "That's right," he agreed.

"Let's fetch the magic lantern along," Rowdy suggested. "B. B. likes to run off at the mouth. Maybe he'll give scientific lectures to the workers on dull evenings, with lantern slides to illustrate them."

Champion cupped his hands to his mouth. "Hey!" he shouted. "Some of you boys climb up here. We've got another one for you to put in the bag."

Workers toiled up the ledge to transport the unconscious Grubb to the canyon floor and add him to their collection of prisoners, large among whom loomed Pocatella. Rowdy looked over this disgruntled group. "With Quong under guard at Hatter's, we've made a good round-up," he observed. "If some of the others got away, let them go. They'll be clearing out of the country fast. The pay window has just closed."

They came back towards the construction camp, a gay group except for the prisoners, who trudged along in the rain, surrounded by Chinese and Irish workers, who gave them a taste of their tongues and an occasional jab with a pick-handle. They came through the night to where the big fires burned. Fresh barrels and boxes were heaped upon the flames. Bartholomew B. Bartholomew and little Launcelot stood waiting; and reports were made, and the prisoners were placed under guard in construction shacks. Someone broached a barrel of whisky, albeit B. B. took a hasty glance over his shoulder to be sure Miss Arabella Hatter hadn't materialised.

Grubb had come to consciousness, and he glared defiantly at his captors. "You still can't prove I killed Big Tom McMasters," he declared.

"You'll talk," Rowdy prophesied. "You'll talk because Quong will talk to try to save that skinny neck of his, and the two of you will hang each other. Some Montana Central men have died. Any Weetigo jury, made up of men who've been hanging Tom McMasters' dummy every year, will decide against you without leaving the box."

After Grubb was hustled away, Bartholomew B. Bartholomew proposed to speak, and a man might as well have tried plugging up a volcano. B. B. led his audience through windy mazes, the Chinese and Irish listening politely if not comprehendingly; and B. B. extolled all those who'd had a part in the night's doings, saying things about Rowdy and Stumpy that were a surprise, even to them. "Montana Central is indebted to you two," B. B. concluded. "*I* am indebted to you. My son, here, is indebted, as his children shall be after him. Mr. Dow, if there is anything your heart desires—*anything*—you have only to name it. I'm sure the Chicago office will concur in my bestowing any favour within my possibilities. Will you speak, sir?"

"Well," said Rowdy, "the man who captured Doctor Quong is really the man who busted up things. That was Stumpy. If you've got any favours to pass out, you'd better pass them to him."

"Ah, Mr. Grampis, a word from you," B. B. insisted. "Will you name a reward of your choosing?"

"Anything, Stumpy," Rowdy reminded his partner.

It took Stumpy a moment to realise the full potentialities here, but opportunity didn't need to jar the door off its hinges for Stumpy to hear the knock. With a bound, he was at B. B.'s side; but it was upon little Launcelot that Stumpy fastened a horny hand. While the multitude waited in astonishment, Stumpy got the squirming, protesting Launcelot across his knee.

"And now, pard," said Stumpy, grinning at Rowdy, "If you'll just be so kind as to hand me the biggest barrel stave you can find, I'll collect the reward."

21 : **One Last Chore**

They sat this sunlit summer morning, did Rowdy and Stumpy, at a corner table in the saloon across from the Odd Fellows building in Tailholt, a pair of men who'd done a good night's work and earned respite. They sat with two tall glasses before them, served by the bartender, who looked as though he were close to tears. Stumpy, too, was saddened as he contemplated his glass and manfully lifted it to his lips from time to time. Lemonade! But a man had to adjust himself to the circumstances that beset him, and Stumpy was valiant. Rowdy, absorbed in thought, paid scant attention to this sorry substitute for liquor. The time had come for a decision.

"Here's how the situation stands," Rowdy said at last. "There are two trains heading out of here this morning. The first is a work train, bound for end-of-steel. The other is going the opposite direction and has a passenger coach. We'd better be on one or the other."

"I been thinkin' about that, too," said Stumpy.

Rowdy shrugged. "Quong's on his way to Hop Gow, under guard. Grubb and Pocatello and most of the railroad raiders are behind bars. The rest have hit the grit. And Hatter has agreed to let the tracks cross his ranch. That means Montana Central won't have a bit of opposition between end-of-steel and Porphyry. Trouble-shooting's going to be a nice soft job from here on out, Stumpy. We'll draw our pay and all we'll have to do is ride around and look wise. Mighty soft, eh?"

"And mighty dull," said Stumpy.

Rowdy sighed. "That's what I was thinking, pard."

"The trouble with us, Rowdy, is that every time we get us a job, we always work ourselves out of it, pronto."

"The better to see what's on the other side of the hill, Stumpy."

That leathery little man contemplated his glass with a frown that should have *sweetened* the lemonade. "Might be nicer towns yonder somewheres."

"We could flip a coin," Rowdy suggested.

"It would likely get lost in a crack in the floor. Me, I vote to draw our pay and head out of here. Shucks, Rowdy, the chores is done."

"That's surely so, pard."

Around them the town hummed, the boots of graders and track-layers beating upon the planking, the boots of miners from Porphyry adding to the steady tattoo above the soft shuffling of Chinese slippers. Sometimes spurs tinkled as cowboys from the far-flung ranches meandered along. Rowdy would never hear the tinkle of spurs without remembering the Sober Swede and the thunder muttering and a dead man awaiting the queer sort of resurrection Big Tom McMasters had had. And then Rowdy was torn from his reverie by the entrance of Miss Arabella Hatter.

She came bustling into the saloon as though the place were on fire and she owned the only bucket in town, a small and sixtyish spinster dressed in a manner that admitted of no nonsense. She stopped in the centre of the sawdust-strewn floor, her bonnet slightly askew, her shrewd blue eyes peering through her square, steel-rimmed spectacles as she surveyed the establishment. Spying Rowdy and Stumpy, she approached their table, sniffing the air as though checking the contents of their glasses. Rowdy toed out a chair for her.

"Sit down," he invited. "Care for a drink? The barkeep can cut it with water if you think it's too strong."

"Why, Mr. Dow," she said, "that's kind of you. But I simply haven't the time. I'm taking the train to the construction camp, you know. Just making my daily check-up to be sure that none of the saloons are forgetting the edict regarding the serving of alcohol."

"You packin' a hatchet in your handbag?" Stumpy wanted to know.

"What a facetious question, Mr. Grampis!" Miss Hatter smiled. "You know how I abhor violence." Her smile became a frown. "Mr. Bartholomew is still at end-of-steel, isn't he?"

"Him and all the others," Stumpy said.

"I simply must see him at once. Do you realise, gentlemen, that a great deal of gambling goes on in Tailholt? I'm told that the Chinese are simply addicted to it. A great many of them have families in China, but not one cent of their pay ever reaches those poor, starving dependents of theirs. Not a cent! It is all squandered on pots and pans— or whatever they call that weird game they play. And some of those heathens probably have several wives in China! Worse pity! Imagine all those poor benighted women having to live on rice while their husband gambles away his wages! Mr. Bartholomew is going to have to do something about this deplorable situation! As a stockholder, I shall insist that he close every gambling establishment at once!"

"Look," said Rowdy, "you came out here to visit your Cousin Lucius, didn't you? Now that that spur business is all settled, don't you think you should be heading for the Hatter ranch?"

"Cousin Lucius," Miss Hatter said sternly, "needs rest. A great deal of it. Such were the doctor's orders. As much as it breaks my heart, I've decided not to trouble the Hatters at all. It simply wouldn't be the thing to do. But while I still have time to spend in the West, it's my bounden duty to crusade against the evils I find."

From the region of the tracks a train bell began its

monotonous clanging, the locomotive's whistle speaking intermittently; and Miss Hatter lifted her head to the sound, for all the world like a fire horse hearing the clarion call. "I'm simply going to have to be running if I'm to be on that work train," she said. "Not another day must pass without my taking up this matter of gambling with Mr. Batholomew."

She left the saloon with a swish of skirts, the batwings creaking behind her; and Rowdy morosely considered his lemonade as though he'd just become aware of it. "Did you say, Stumpy," he asked, "that all the chores were done?"

"It was you, Rowdy, that said Montana Central wouldn't be having no more opposition."

Rowdy sighed.

"One last chore, confound her," Stumpy muttered.

Rowdy, deep in thought again, brightened, then beckoned to the bartender. "Pencil and paper," Rowdy ordered; and these things were brought to him. "You ain't the first gent to ask," the bartender said. "More than one has drawed up his will after tasting that stuff we're serving now."

Rowdy fell to scribbling, then glanced at his partner. "Do you remember the name of Miss Hatter's room-mate, Stumpy? That other teacher she was talking about on the stagecoach?"

"Mathilda," Stumpy said promptly. "Never forgot it on account of I once knew a calf had the same name. A ornery critter it was, too."

Rowdy continued writing, then held up his accomplishment for Stumpy to see. "We'll have the telegrapher send this out to end-of-steel," Rowdy explained. "She won't know but what it came from New Hampshire. All telegrams are relayed out of Tailholt over the railroad wire."

The message read:

MISS ARABELLA HATTER,

TAILHOLT, MONTANA

DESPERATELY URGENT THAT YOU HURRY BACK AS SOON AS POSSIBLE STOP SCHOOL BOARD MAKING RULING TO RETIRE ALL TEACHERS OVER THIRTY ON GROUNDS THAT THOSE OLDER ARE FIT ONLY FOR BONEYARD STOP WE NEED YOU TO LEAD FIGHT AGAINST THIS OUTRAGE STOP WITHOUT YOU WE ARE LOST.

MATHILDA

"That should have her packin' her bag," Stumpy chuckled. "Ain't a question or a doubt. Rowdy, you've really earned your pay. You've just rid Montana Central of the last of its obstacles."

"I'll pick up our pay and file this on the way to the tracks," Rowdy said. "You get our things from the Traveller's Rest, Stumpy. I'll meet you aboard that train that's heading east from here."

"What's the name of that town where we left our private hosses when we decided to take the stagecoach to Tailholt, Rowdy?"

"We'll find it, pard."

And so it came about that before the morning was over, that trouble-shooting team, Rowdy and Stumpy, were hunkered down in seats aboard a passenger coach, awaiting the train's departure, an unemployed pair. From the window they could see Tailholt, and Rowdy's face softened as he had his look.

Always there was this moment when a job was done and a man had only his remembrances. But Rowdy was thinking of Mad Hatter as he'd last seen him, a man restored to wholeness, a man who'd shaken Rowdy's hand and thanked him for the part the partners had played in his recovery. And he was thinking of Mark Champion and Taisy who had been making talk of a wedding to be held at Porphyry when the last rail was laid. They'd wanted Rowdy at that wedding, but Rowdy had made them no promise. He sighed now. She was quite a gal, that Taisy.

And there was Avalanche McAllister to remember, too, a man who did his duty by his job and had shared the dangers of that wild ride through the storm with Rowdy and Stumpy. And Bartholomew B. Bartholomew who had promised that Montana Central would do anything for the men who had saved the railroad and had been as good as his word. And there was that dead man, Tom McMasters, who would no longer be hanged in effigy, and his daughter, who was now proud of her father's name. And Hop Gow, who had proved himself a friend in need and would be repaid. Of such things were remembrances made, and these were the debits to be entered in the ledger of a man's living to strike the right kind of balance. Yes, Rowdy reflected, he and Stumpy had done more than help build a railroad spur in the Weetigo country. Rowdy was satisfied.

And Stumpy? The train lurched to a sudden start and began moving; Tailholt fell behind and the adventure was ended; and Stumpy fell to massaging his right arm—the arm that had wielded a barrel stave against the posterior of little Launcelot Bartholomew last night.

"Your arm numb, partner?" Rowdy inquired.

"Mighty numb," said Stumpy, rubbing the harder.

And Stumpy smiled. . . .